IN THE FLESH

In the Flesh

A NOVEL BY

Christa Wolf

Translated from the German

by John S. Barrett

A VERBA MUNDI BOOK

David R. Godine · Publisher · Boston

This is
A Verba Mundi Book
published in 2005 by
David R. Godine, Publisher
Post Office Box 450
Jaffrey, New Hampshire 03452
www.godine.com

LIBRARY OF CONGRESS
CATALOGING-IN-PUBLICATION DATA

Wolf, Christa.
[Leibhaftig. English]
In the flesh : a novel by Christa Wolf ;
translated from the German by John S. Barrett.— 1st ed.
    p.   cm.
ISBN 1-56792-267-8 (hardcover : alk. paper)
ISBN 1-56792-291-0 (paperback : alk. paper)
I. Barrett, John S. (John Smith), 1935– II. Title.
PT2685.036L3613   2005
833'.914—dc22
2004019882

First Edition
PRINTED IN THE UNITED STATES OF AMERICA

IN THE FLESH

Hurting.

Something's complaining, wordlessly. Words breaking against the muteness that's spreading persistently, along with faintness. Consciousness bobbing up and down in a primordial tide. Her memories like islands. Wherever it's carrying her now, words don't reach – that would be one of her last clear thoughts. It's complaining. In her, around her. No one there to hear the complaint. Just the incoming tide and the spirit above the waters. An odd way to envision it. From long-practiced politeness, she whispers – with her thick, paralyzed tongue – that ambulances are so bouncy. A comment that the physician sitting on the folding seat next to her stretcher picks up enthusiastically, strangely delighted. A disgraceful situation, he couldn't agree more, an absolute disgrace, but all their protests have been to no avail. Then he reminds her not to move her left arm. From the transparent container above her, jiggling in time with the ambulance, drop after drop is flowing through a tube and into a vein. Elixir. The elixir of life. With her right hand she has to hold on to the trapeze hanging from the vehicle's ceiling so as not to be shaken off the hard stretcher. The pain from her incision increases. "No wonder, considering the circumstances," says the physician grimly. A long ride. Rising and falling. Sinking away. And the complaining is becoming more insistent. A downward journey. A big, new wave from the same tide, taking me with it. Going under. Being pulled under. Dark, still.

That voice. Annoying. Two syllables, repeated persistently, that are starting to seem familiar to her. A name. Her name. Why's he calling me by my first name? A young man's face, framed by a narrow strip of beard. Right above her. Too close to her. He calls that name over and over, demandingly, too loudly. It's disturbing her. What does he want? She ought to answer, but can't. With some effort, she can nod. Finally he leaves her alone – she's understood. Nothing's shaking anymore. With her fingertips she explores what's beneath her. Soft. Above her, two I.V. bottles. A whitewashed ceiling. A room, a white room. She takes it to be some sort of waiting room, noisy, drafty. She shuts her eyes and falls into her gray-black inner room, hovers above the still waters. Man's life resembles the waters. "C'mon, stay awake." Annoying. She sinks. A beating from inside startles her, she doesn't recognize it right away. That's her heart beating that way! At a gallop. Someone's yelling. Again. Summon all your strength, open your eyes. The face of a very young woman, a pink gown. She forms, probably inaudibly, a few words, the word "heart" comes out, but the girl doesn't understand. Painfully slowly, she feels for her pulse. "Doctor! Tachycardia!" Your face, all of a sudden, next to the face of the much too young doctor. What do you want, where did you come from? She thinks she ought to feel something. Are you saying something? I'm sinking. My heart is racing. I hear words. "Pulse rate." "Paroxysmal." They barely touch the outer limits of her consciousness. I'm sinking past my mother's face as she lies near death. I'm standing by the window of her hospital room and seeing myself through her eyes – a black silhouette against the summer light. I hear myself saying, "They've marched into Prague." And hear

4

my mother whisper, "There are worse things." She turns her head toward the wall. "There are worse things." She dies. I think of Prague.

Amazing that there are so many interior rooms. Now she glides into one of them, where bad things are happening. Hellish noise, revolting noise overwhelms everything, from somewhere far away she feels the urge to complain, but the urge lacks the anger needed to propel it. Instead, someone wants to know what medicine he should inject. "What medicine are you taking?" he screams. "Try to remember." She's flung upward, opens her eyes. Too much light. The doctor's mouth forms a name that doesn't seem familiar to her, she shakes her head no. She hears "Let's try it." He doesn't seem to be very sure of himself. What are you doing? says your voice. What do you mean? She listens hard to the question. "Don't get upset, we'll soon have it under control."

I'm not getting upset at all. She wouldn't even have the strength to get upset. "It's quite unpleasant," somebody once told her, "but you don't die of it." That was during the first episode, it was the lady doctor in the walk-in clinic at the film studio, you weren't there, our film was supposed to be "previewed and approved." Those were words of betrayal as far as I was concerned, but Lothar calmed me down. We were sitting on a bench under a birch tree in front of the studio. "It'll all work out okay," Lothar assured me. "Now's exactly the right time for a film like this one – the public's ripe for it and at the moment the higher-ups aren't interested in getting into a hassle with the artists." At that point my heartbeat went out of kilter. Did I really believe, I heard Lothar saying, and laughing at the same time, that he'd let them tear us to shreds? And I said, "I can't go to the preview." His laughter broke off. He took it as cowardice, as lack of faith in his ability to stand up to them. He was insulted,

CRISTA WOLF

I could tell by that expression on his face. "Feel my pulse," I said. He did it reluctantly, was shocked, and took me to the clinic himself – considerate, as he could be at such moments. Two feelings at odds within me, I can still remember that much, my memory's best when it comes to contradictory feelings. I didn't like it at all that I'd collapsed there in front of everyone and let them see what was going on inside me. I was afraid, it was just now becoming clear to me. But on the other hand it was also just fine that I wouldn't be able to go to the preview, that was obvious, Lothar kept repeating that. "We'll just take care of it ourselves, that'll be even better." Deep within me, someone was giggling with me, at me.

The doctor is still trying to get through to her. The injection didn't work, that was to be expected. She's got to try harder to remember what the right drug was. So you told them that those attacks were coming more often and that there's an effective medicine but you don't know the name, because you can't bring yourself to pay attention to such things. I hear you saying, "Try to think back." It's as if you're mad at me because I'm so forgetful. It has to come back to her. In this emergency her brain can just call off its general strike. In her mind's eye she can see the box that contains the medication: it's pale green, the lettering on it is white. Now she can read off the name. Whispering, she passes it on to the young doctor who has the emergency duty, takes care of the emergency cases, he repeats the name in a loud voice, questioningly, she lowers and raises her eyelids in confirmation. The doctor has figured out how to make himself understood, now he seems pleased with her, she hears him give an order to the nurse. "Do we have it here?" "We do." "That's good!"

I was sick back then, too, a little anyway, nothing to

compare with today, but I wasn't putting on or exaggerating, I did need Lothar's arm, I couldn't walk any faster, I was having trouble breathing, but at the same time it struck me that his assistance was more official in nature, less personal, though his exaggerated chivalry smoothed over a situation that was painful for us both. And I was also struck that he was even taking care of this situation officially, getting a hint of that self-important expression on his face that you knew to expect under such (fortunately fairly rare) circumstances. And that in the clinic he exuded that reserved but unmistakable authority, with just the right little doses of sharpness that got the nurse at the reception desk moving and then the doctor as well. Did I ever tell you about that? Funny, it all suddenly struck me as I was lying down on the hard examining table and I asked myself where and when Lothar could have learned all that. He hadn't by the time we were students together. I tried hard to downplay my weakness, even forced a grin, although I was a little upset, just a little, a sort of agitation that was still manageable but which would increase somewhat over the next two hours, I never told you about it, but it was a long way from deserving the name "fear of death," which the lady doctor brought up in the form of a question. "No fear of death? No?" No. So, fear of death was one of the symptoms you had to have with a rapid heartbeat? "Oh, I see, you don't even know the expression."

Now she knows it but doesn't need it. She's still not afraid of death, presumably too weak for that. And she's not really upset that this injection isn't working, either, after all she's a pro as far as these attacks are concerned, a doctor even agreed with her recently. That first attack came over me unexpectedly, catching me unprepared, innocent – just in case that word might be appropriate here – not putting on, and back then I didn't have any idea of what it meant when it persisted obstinately for an hour, then a second hour, until the lady doctor sent to the druggist for a stronger medication that she didn't have on hand. Lothar looked in – he was the only one who was permitted to look in, it was a privilege of his rank – and announced that everything was being done. As if she could have had the slightest doubt about it. She was becoming well acquainted with the bright, antiseptic room in which she was lying, the row of glass cabinets along the wall with instruments and boxes of medicines, the big window that looked out onto the green. The tops of birches in the wind – that made her feel good, now the word has lost all its meaning for me, feeling good, I can't even imagine it, why are you looking at me that way?

Lothar offered his services to the lady doctor firmly, but at the same time, reassuringly. Should he send a car, see about getting a more effective drug, perhaps one that we don't have here? Bring in a specialist for consultation? Don't want to miss anything. His behaving like such a big shot was painful for me, seemed to be for the doctor as well, who answered in monosyllables. There had been an aura of insincerity about him, for how long? "Falseness," a hard word, you used it once, not in reference to Lothar, but to Urban, a lot later I believe. How'd I get onto Urban? You were pretty observant about whatever involved him. Too observant, I told you, we both knew what I meant by that. You shrugged your shoulders. Words like "jealousy" didn't come up between us. "Anyway," said Lothar, "I've come straight from the preview. I'll just say congratulations."

At that point I asked myself whether my body, whose tricks I was beginning to figure out, had simply staged the whole business so I could be completely indifferent to such a statement from Lothar. "One more thing," said Lothar, "Urban called." Funny how he kept his self-important expression when he talked about people in authority. We'd always teased him about it. Urban, in particular, never missed a chance. "Attention everyone, on your feet, Lothar's getting serious." Funny that Urban had now become an authority figure for Lothar. When did that happen? Was it just that Urban had been promoted over Lothar and was now in a position to give him orders and pass judgment on his work? Mild judgment if at all possible or, if criticism was unavoidable, criticism cloaked in irony that always made it evident that we'd all been hatched in the same incubator, as Urban put it. That reassurance, even when not expressed in so many words, was important for Lothar. And that Urban had called right away to find out how the preview had gone. That he'd been really gratified by the favorable outcome. That he was concerned about me and sent his regards.

"We're not getting anywhere this way," says the young doctor. In the meantime, she's been hooked up to a monitor that displays her electrocardiogram on a screen. A painfully thin woman doctor, who must have come in without her having noticed, is fiddling with the apparatus. She has graying hair that's cut so that it looks like a tight-fitting cap. "Really high pulse rate," she says disapprovingly, the young physician with the strip of beard around his cheeks and chin doesn't like that a bit and begins to list all the things he's tried, as if to defend himself. She'd like to take his side. The woman doctor, who seems to be in charge now, names a medication. Does she know it? She has to answer in the negative. "It's new," says the woman doctor. "We inject it very carefully, under monitor control. But you're soaking wet!" A short back and forth between her and the blond nurse in the pink gown. No, they can't change me here in the emergency ward, they'll do it as soon as I'm admitted to a room.

The lady doctor in the walk-in clinic wiped my face with

a tissue, I can still recall that, but I don't remember what she looked like, faces get away from me, a shortcoming that's still incomprehensible to you. Lothar, however, suddenly dropped his phony look and put on his old-friend expression. I do still remember that. Worried, embarrassed, didn't know what to do, just the way a man acts when confronted by a woman's illness. I had to smile, smile at him, which seemed to relieve him.

"Any chance you can bear down for us?" asks the gaunt woman doctor, at which point the young doctor reproachfully displays the patient's abdominal incision to her, that's got to be where the primary problem is, but the woman doctor won't give up, with her thumb she presses firmly on the artery in the neck, but even that doesn't slow the pulse. "Ice water?" "She can't take anything by mouth." "Oh, right." Now she's alienated the gaunt woman doctor as well.

My runaway body. Metaphorically. All that's transitory is just a metaphor. Some of those lines she'd never really understood, their meaning remained hidden from her in a seemingly porous but impenetrable darkness until today, until this dark moment when the meaning suddenly dawns on her. When, however, the hundred years have finally passed, every hedge of thorns lies down, Theseus holds the thread of Ariadne tightly in his hand and finds his way safely out of the labyrinth, every secret reveals itself if you keep at it long enough. Whether you believe me or not, I still remember what was going through my head back then in the studio's walk-in clinic, I was only in my mid-thirties, young, so young, time seemed to stretch out, my heart was racing just like now. "Afraid?" "Yes." "Afraid of death?" "No." "That's unusual."

Now the gaunt woman doctor is trying to chase someone away from the door, but he comes in anyway. Well, it's you, where've you been so long? I try to greet you with my eyes, but I don't know, of course, whether you'll understand my eye signals right away, you're talking with the doctors. She has to remember that you can be too weak to be glad about something and that nobody in the world can know that besides you, yourself. Now the woman doctor sits down on the edge of the bed, feels the vein in the hollow in front of her right elbow, orders her to make a fist. "Squeeze harder!" and, almost unnoticed by her, inserts the needle into the vein and begins, in slow motion, to push down the plunger of the syringe. She pauses now and then. She keeps her eyes on the green zigzag line on the oscilloscope, her heart rate. With her eyes she communicates with the young doctor standing on the other side of the bed. They both shake their heads almost imperceptibly. Her heart is racing. "Are you still with us?"

Or couldn't it be that my heart, given the choice between stopping entirely and galloping away, has decided to gallop away? For my benefit, as it were? Not that she'd think up such questions, they just ask themselves. Everything around her, that cold, inhospitable room, those machines hooked to her by tubes and wires, the pulse that won't slow down even after the woman physician has resolutely squeezed the last drop out of the syringe and into her venous system, all that expresses the questions she can't put into words. Go away, I tell you, please just go away. I'm getting worked up because you're here. Please go. She has to remind herself that it can be too much of a strain when the closest person in the same room is just like you.

How long did it take for my pulse to slow down back then? More than two hours, I think. Our film had been shown long since, it was a hit, as Lothar kept reassuring me repeatedly. As far as anyone could see, there would be no problems with approval. The doctor had instructions to call him when I was "fit to travel." He'd ordered an official car for me and I was really glad not to have to climb up the steps into the bus. I was exhausted, exhausted in a not unpleasant way, no wonder, I heard, my heart had just run a marathon. I was alone at home and had a good, deep sleep. Urban was the first one who called me the following morning and I thanked him sincerely for being so considerate. But the sincerity soon petered out on both sides, I have to admit. You always think that when the other person's not entirely sincere, you have the right to pretend a little. Our pretending consisted of the fact – do you still remember? – that for a long time we acted as if we still believed in Urban's sincerity. Arguments about the film started almost immediately. Lothar didn't offer his congratulations about it again, but he didn't give up on it entirely, either. He made himself – and we held that in his favor – into a buffer. But when the attacks were directed even at him, he began to discreetly distance himself from the film, not from us, not that. The most derogatory remarks he didn't pass on to us. He kept quiet as long as he could. We never found out from him that even Urban was putting pressure on him. He'd said that he didn't doubt the subjective honesty of our intent, but that the objective effect of the film, given the current situation, was, well, ambiguous. That opinion Lothar eventually shared with us as his own opinion. He looked right through us. But that's all so long ago, twenty-five years, a quarter of a century. It's all become so inconceivable. And hadn't they lost Urban even earlier? How often in the course of a lifetime do we turn into someone else and lose those with whom we were young and, well, yes, innocent?

Night. Something like night, only deeper, darker, more lonely. Later, she will not remember this most night-filled of all nights, only her recollection of it. Somehow they must have managed to get her heart rate under control. Admitted her and put her in a bed. She's in a room, a room with a window from which something like a glow is coming, the premonition of a glow. Her gown is still wet, the bedclothes as well. As she awakens, an ear-splitting din starts, a shrill clattering, never heard before, as if metal objects were being beaten against each other, smashed together with brutal force, lances, swords. She sees bodies fighting each other, knotted together in contorted, unnatural poses. That's not funny, someone's getting serious with me. If I'd ever thought that I was lost, I can't have known what the word means. A hellish screeching and shrieking and yelling that goes right to your very bones, a roaring and hammering and hissing that goes beyond the boundaries of pain. I never dreamed there could be such sounds, nobody could. Or that they could be put to use as torture. That's how far we've come. In that sick, greenish-blue light from an unknown source, in the midst of that hellish racket, I am tormented by the history of pain and torture. The soldiers of Herod who impale tiny children on the points of their swords. The first Christians in the arena, eye to eye with wild beasts that roar hideously while tearing them apart. The atrocities of the conquistadores, the crusaders, the princes after the peasants' revolt. The woman, battered, floating in the Landwehr Canal. And my century was just getting started. Every imaginable variation on the slaughterhouse. The martyrdom and destruction of bodies, my body among them. There are intervals of merciful unconsciousness – whether minutes or seconds she doesn't know.

"Are you in pain?" She must have given the wrong answer or none at all. The nurse has gone away.

"Everything has its price" is a cliché, she knows that, but

13

like all clichés it remains one only as long as it's not being inscribed on your own flesh. The price for the fact that something is ending in this bed and that thereafter – should there be a thereafter – something else will begin, is that horrible noise and the bodily torments that are being burned into my mind for some reason. The pillories in which women are displayed in the marketplace. The racks and thumbscrews, the glowing tongs, the ducking stools. Drawing and quartering with the help of horses, breaking on the wheel, hanging, drowning, burying alive. Rape. Now revenge is being extracted for the fact that ever since she was a child, she'd just quickly skimmed over the portrayals of all those horrors, closed her eyes in the movies, left the room when such things started up again on television. For the fact that she'd only been in what used to be a concentration camp a single time. Again and again she has to walk through the same concrete-lined, poorly lighted corridor, which she thinks she knows but cannot place. Which she's driven back into whenever she gets close to the exit. My premonition that I'll meet up with you behind the heavy steel gates is choked off each time. What does it mean that I'm looking for the exit from that subterranean labyrinth where I'm hoping to find you as well? The noise turns into the rattling of chains, the chains of countless prisoners.

Sometime it becomes morning again. A doctor appears, a man of average build whom the nurse accompanying him – yet another one, plumpish – addresses as Herr Chefarzt, the chief of surgery. He wants to know how things are going for her. Does he really want to know? She doesn't know him, didn't understand his name, couldn't answer anyway. He seems to realize that her parched mouth can't form any words. He moistens her lips and mouth with a cotton swab. Then she can say, "Why do I feel so bad?"

Contrary to expectation, the Chefarzt takes the question seriously, doesn't even seem to be surprised by it, doesn't feel annoyed. "Because you're lacking in most vital elements," he says. "Potassium, for instance. Your blood tests show that you hardly even have any potassium. Your magnesium's low. Calcium. Iron. Phosphorus. Zinc. All the minerals. The first thing we have to do is build you up gradually."

Information that sheds some light, that she'll have to think about for a while. She asks herself in passing who inside of her might be eating up her potassium and the other "elements," a term like "killer cells" sneaks through her mind, but she really doesn't want to know. The man whom the nurse calls Chefarzt seems not to want to tell her more than she really wants to know. He starts to put on plastic gloves. Two pairs tear and they don't have a third pair in his size. Controlling himself, he says, "Please be so kind as to get some more, Sister Margot, thanks." When the third pair of gloves remains intact, he removes the dressing from her abdomen, cleans the incision, re-dresses it with the help of the nurse. He asks about her temperature. With an impenetrable expression, the nurse hands him the chart. He says formally, "We have to be patient. I'll be back soon."

That's a statement she can depend on. Two bouncy young nurses go about washing her, conversing at the same time about the intolerable traffic conditions in the city. Somewhere in this world, maybe even quite close by, the streetcars are still running, but much too infrequently, so that one of the nurses, the small blond one, constantly arrives late for the early shift and gets chewed out by the head nurse. But who can expect her to get up a half hour earlier just because of the stupid streetcar?

In the meantime, there are tubes coming out of my belly that end in containers on the floor to the right of my bed.

15

How shocked I was once when I saw a friend lying there like that. I wouldn't be shocked now. So people aren't right when they say that the things that shock you most are the ones that directly affect you. Of course everything could be totally different, depending on whether you have enough potassium or not. Those columns of prisoners who are again passing by can summon up the will to survive if they just have enough potassium. But they give up when they're low on all the minerals. Are called mussulmen when they get to the point of apathy. Without potassium – now I could tell the Chefarzt if he'd moisten my mouth again, which the young nurses have forgotten about, despite his request – without potassium you feel like a toad pinned to the ground by a forked stick against the back of its neck.

It's an apt image, earlier an apt image would have been really satisfying to her, now she doesn't care. The noise has started up again. The columns dragging themselves through a desolate landscape are rattling their chains. It strikes her that each person is punished through whichever sense is most acute, hearing in my case, and the fear of physical pain that even as a child – did I ever tell you about that? – led me to submit to tests of pain and courage, which won me a reputation for bravery.

How would we know how extensive our interior world is if there weren't special keys – high fever, for example – to unlock it for us? She keeps having to go through that low, poorly lighted, and poorly ventilated corridor, which seems familiar to her each time but which she can't summon up the strength to really recognize. Still, she must have previously seen those figures in dark gray fatigues that are now demanding her papers by gestures that aren't at all overbearing, just matter-of-fact gestures that put her into a paroxysm of fear. So you have to identify yourself even here, but what does she mean by "here"? She finds a card in her pocket, a little piece of cardboard whose inadequacy is immediately obvious, but the two – attendants? guards? inspectors? – wave her through. They couldn't have made themselves understood any other way down here because of the hellish noise that never lets up.

There's no doubt whatsoever that she's down below. The steel doors open quite easily, gliding soundlessly on their hinges and rails, if a word like "soundlessly" has any sense in the midst of such a din. Quite easily she wanders or glides through a number of vast rooms that are crammed together, that merge with one another, and now she understands, too, why people speak of the "realm of shadows," call the netherworld the realm of shadows, and why the recently deceased are spoken of as "shades." But we should really stop pitying them because they can see and hear, they just don't feel anything. At least one who's temporarily sent off in their company doesn't feel anything – that I can attest to.

But of course you know very well that we once met each other in those corridors, Urban and I, in that earthly realm of shadows that's not identical to the underworld in the hereafter but that does have its similarities, that earthly transit passageway that's tiled like a bathhouse. Or like a slaughterhouse. Disguised as a border crossing – the "frontier" railroad station on Friedrichstrasse. Urban had come on the same commuter train as I did, Zoo Station to Friedrichstrasse, the same human torrent had sluiced him down the stairs and along that subterranean passageway up to the point where the stream divided into travelers who wanted to enter the state of which we were citizens, whose territory began at that spot, and those with the usual travel permits who were returning to that state, many older people among them. And finally, the trickle of diplomats and people on official business trips, the group to which we both belonged, Urban and I. We were permitted, or obliged, to go straight through, and that's where I first recognized him, right in front of me, it was too late to let myself drift back, I could tell by his stiff back that he'd seen me, too. So we literally bumped into each other in front of the passport inspection booth, feigning happy surprise over the way chance had brought us together at that very place – after so many years! We started right off counting them. Not a place you like to meet people. You don't like to let anyone else get a look at the documents that allow you to temporarily shift from one world to another. You immediately fall prey to the compulsion to justify yourselves to each other, to quickly tell about the urgent business, work, or mission you had to take care of "over there," smiling ironically and watching out of the corner of your eye as your "travel document" is taken by one of the men in uniform, after he's compared you with the passport picture, and then pushed through the slit into the inspection booth where, carefully shielded from sight, there's another uniformed man who puts your papers through some sort of procedure that remains hidden from the people waiting outside – except for the fact that, regardless, people can draw their own conclusions about how irreproachable or suspicious you are in the eyes of the authorities by how long your papers spend inside that little building.

My friend Urban was one of the irreproachable. He'd just started, with a suitable leavening of self-deprecation, to tell about the conference in the other part of the city, at which he – as a regular guest, he considered that a feather in his cap – had to make a presentation about the most recent cultural events in our country, when we heard the stamper banging down on the other side of the opaque glass and then his documents appeared in the slit under the window, were picked up by the first man in uniform and, after he'd again compared the passport photo with the real article, were handed back to Urban. He accepted them not entirely without pride. "You can at least depend on those computers!" And then, like a loyal colleague, he waited a considerable time for her beyond the customs inspection point, which he'd also passed through without delay. Yep, you could depend on those computers, they'd obviously stored instructions for the uniformed men at the crossing point to delay her entry, even to telephone their superiors to assure themselves that there was nothing suspicious about her papers, she told Urban that when she finally caught up with him, passing through customs as uneventfully as he had. His smile was a bit forced – of course he felt a perverse sort of envy over the fact that the computers had kept her from passing through as smoothly as he had, but on the other hand, it would have disturbed him if he'd had to wait as long for his papers as she did. Their ways parted right in front of the exit from the building, unique in all the world for having been constructed right over the entrance to and egress from a competing world. Her old friend Urban walked over to the taxi stand in front of the Friedrichstrasse Commuter Station. She turned to the left toward the Weidendamm Bridge, which I never cross without sneering at the cast-iron Prussian eagle on the railing, or at least touching it.

I hadn't asked Urban what his position was then – he obviously assumed that I'd been following his career as it led him logically, step by step, upwards from a beginning that seemed convincing and straightforward to all of us but then, at some point, was lost to sight and went on its way behind the scenes, apparently successfully. I didn't turn around, but I could feel in my back that he was watching me as I walked away.

If you live long enough, situations repeat themselves, sometimes, however, by showing up in reverse. Once, years ago, I'd watched him – it must have been after a conference – as he disappeared down the stairs feigning haste, without saying goodbye to her, she'd forgotten the reason, only that he was embarrassed to be seen with her because of some incident or other, at least he wanted to get away from her. Yes, she'd watched him for a long time back then and was aware of a sinking feeling.

How was she feeling now? She'd have to go on giving the Chefarzt the same answer: like I'm at the bottom of a mineshaft that I can't get out of because I don't have enough strength. She says, "I'm getting along okay." He seems to place less weight on what she has to say than on the results of his own examination. He feels her abdomen, takes her pulse, pulls up her eyelids, then even wants to know her most recent temperature, at which point Christine, the nurse on duty, is forced to remind him that temperatures are only taken twice daily, whereupon the head surgeon gives the order to take this patient's temperature every three hours. "If you'd be so kind," he says to the nurse, who has pretty blond hair that curls around her face. She takes down the order without commenting. But she's insulted, she can't hide the traces of it around the corners of her mouth. "What's wrong, Sister Christine?" says the Chefarzt. He learns that the floor is understaffed. She, who can hardly speak but can still hear quite well, isn't interested in knowing how patient care is going to be compromised by that fact and is grateful to the Chefarzt for indicating to the nurse that she should talk to him about that later. For the patient he prescribes a sensational novelty: she can have "some sips" of tea. Immediately the mirage of a gigantic glass of beer appears in front of her, the white foam spills temptingly over the rim, she can't manage to suppress the apparition. She waits for her tea and asks herself whether any of the nurses she hears chatting and laughing while pushing beds along the corridor can imagine what every minute that she has to wait for the tea means to her. Then one of the two young ones – the pretty brunette with the birthmark on her left cheek – brings the cup, puts it down smartly on the bedside table, and disappears. She seems not to be concerned about whether the thirsty woman can reach the table with her right hand or whether she can raise her head far enough to drink out of the cup. To her good fortune a young man with a crew cut wearing a white coat comes in and notices her struggling. He says "Humph," goes out and comes back in after a few seconds with a cup with a spout, pours the tea into it, supports her head and holds the cup. "It works a lot better this way, doesn't it?" She drinks. In this world there's not just the word, there's the real thing, drinking. "Thank you," she says. "Evelyn is still a student," he says. "Second year. There're still a lot of things you don't notice." His name is Jürgen, in his third year of his nursing internship, just about to take his licensing exams. He tells her it's all right that she can't get down more than three swallows. "You'd never believe," he says, "how quickly your stomach shrinks." He leaves.

The tide is rising again. It has a name: exhaustion. Consciousness recedes, hits bottom. Hits the dirt. Now it's airplanes making the ear-shattering noise. An unbroken formation of them, coming in at low level, right over our heads. There has to be some hidden meaning to the fact that every variety of human victimhood is being paraded past me. Or is the point of it to convince me finally, after all these years, all the decades of self-deception, of the pervasive senselessness of everything that happens? It's been beaten into our heads that each and every thing becomes sensible, reveals its inner sense, by virtue of the fact that it can be told as history. I begin to suspect which sources are providing the images I'm being forced to watch as soon as the director on my internal stage is put out of action.

Tell me, please, since you're suddenly here again, what time of day is it anyway? Afternoon? I'm amazed. Would you bring me the little blue book with the Goethe poems? First thing tomorrow. But I see you have something else in mind. So you've spoken with the head surgeon behind my back. Says he's not quite happy with my temperature. He thinks it'll be necessary to operate again to get rid of the abscess that's causing this fever.

Give me a little drink, please. This time she manages four swallows of tea. Funny, all that comes to mind are Goethe's poems. Which one do you want to hear? you say. Oh, especially the one that goes "The future veils / happiness and pain / from our gaze at each step / but undaunted / we make our way forward . . ." but I don't know how it goes on from there. Something about "crowns" comes next. I need the book.

Do you know that I actually called Konrad once when I couldn't find that poem? Of all our friends, he was the one who remembered every poem he'd ever read, and he'd read a lot. It hadn't occurred to me to look for it among the "Masonic Songs," but Konrad knew right away, he knew it by heart and told me about Goethe's relationship to the Freemasons. In our first Goethe seminar at Jena he was the one who set the tone, and he was also the one who helped put on the exhibition "Society and Culture in the Age of Goethe" in the palace at Weimar. And sometimes he couldn't talk about anything else when he walked me back to my little room in the Nietzsche House. Nothing was more fascinating, he said, than investigating the ways certain social circumstances fettered genius and what methods genius developed to free itself from those fetters, at least temporarily or partially.

Funny, the way the brain works. Why am I thinking about Konrad now? He was honorable, I have to say, he couldn't do anything that went against his convictions. Wouldn't even say anything against his convictions. He'd still be our friend today, don't you think so? He died too soon. Yes, you say distractedly, but I can't worry about that now. You brought my little black radio along, you plug it in to try it out, a man's voice is giving the news, another airliner has crashed, the number of victims is – for God's sake, I say, turn it off. Yes, yes, okay, you say. But what's wrong? Nothing. Nothing other than the fact that I can't bear even the smallest bit of bad news, do you understand? Okay, okay, you say.

Now leave, please, I say. You say, Just close your eyes. Don't pay any attention to me. I try. Then the noise starts up again. Leave. Maybe later I'll wonder why I wasn't able to bear your presence for more than half an hour. Right now I don't have the strength to wonder. Or even bear a hint of bad news. I have to remember that there's a degree of weakness where you can't take on another milligram of worry or pity for people far away, to say nothing of people who are right nearby. Helene has a cough – you shouldn't have told me that, even though I realized perfectly well that you did it out of embarrassment because, after the way I begged you not to tell me anything bad, you really didn't know what to talk about, and anyway, it's not all that bad when a five-year-old child has a cough, but I can't do anything about the fact that little Helene coughs and coughs, that she's certain to get bronchitis, which can easily become chronic, with all those bad aftereffects, and while bad aftereffects are spreading all through me, that airliner is plunging out of the sky over

23

and over again at the same time, with its still living, but now, a fraction of a second later, its pulverized, crushed, burned, shredded human freight, and all I can do is hope that no one I love, or even just know, is forced, or is foolish enough, to fly in an airplane in the near future, and if anyone does anyway, I don't want to know about it, just as I don't want to know what time you're going to visit tomorrow, because then I'd have to figure out what time you're going to leave and spend an hour on roads that are certainly not overcrowded, to be sure, but not without danger. Just the way – that's something I now know as well – I wouldn't want to know if I had cancer. I want to make a mental note that you can't tell people who've just been operated on and are still very weak that they have cancer – no matter what they may have claimed beforehand. There are circumstances, in other words, in which honesty and truthfulness can have a fatal effect.

When I get the chance, I want to tell that to the Chefarzt, who's just coming back to let her know that they're all agreed that she needs to be operated on again. Before that, however, sometime today – or to be precise, immediately – they'll have to do another test on her. To delineate the abscess that has to be cleaned out. They've just recently acquired an extremely accurate and easily tolerated method for doing that, says the Chefarzt, all the while feeling the pulse at her wrist. She asks herself for the first time how old he might be. It really has to be a good sign that I'm beginning to be interested – even if it's not a burning interest – in the age of the doctor who most assuredly had the deciding vote in the committee that's apparently met to deliberate about my case. In every committee of which I, myself, have been a member, there's always been someone who's had the deciding vote, rarely, very rarely, a woman, and it occurs to me that I've scarcely ever had the deciding vote, fortunately enough. Urban, however, my friend and colleague Urban, had the deciding vote in at least three committees to which I belonged. In the first one, he was unsure of himself and used it clumsily, he could be influenced by argument at that point, and I was satisfied with him. In the second, a routine crept into the way he led discussions, and in the third he didn't even bother to use his power to influence the decision, he began to stifle opposition, and I began to avoid the meetings. Nothing to brag about. How long ago that all is. How deeply submerged.

In the meantime, the Chefarzt has left and Jürgen, the male nurse, has come in with a bottle containing a liter of fluid she's supposed to drink in the next fifteen minutes in preparation for the CAT scan. But I can't. You know that, five swallows of tea was all I could get down. Unconvinced, Jürgen says, "You have to. It's a contrast medium." She breaks out in a sweat. After the first gulps she's wringing wet, but since she's gotten to know how bad the laundry situation is on the floor, she'll resist asking for yet another clean gown and concentrate on swallowing this awful-tasting liquid. What they're expecting of me is impossible, Jürgen knows it, too, he holds the cup with the spout up to her mouth, one more swallow, one more, good, good. Regression to childhood, I was free of responsibilities then, too, just like now, when no one's demanding anything of me except that I behave cooperatively, as the nurse in charge put it: "Now you are cooperative, aren't you?" and I'm embarrassed to say I really felt a twinge of obligation to live up to her expectations, but I can't empty that container, she pushes the last cupful away. Jürgen empties the contents into the sink without a word. Unfortunately, he says, he doesn't have time to accompany her downstairs, into the cellar, the underworld.

25

He's not unintelligent, he's thinking about working as a nurse for a year or two after his exams and then having himself nominated by the hospital to study medicine.

Sister Evelyn doesn't have that kind of ambition. Her main efforts are directed toward looking her best – the strands of her jet-black hair are carefully draped around her head, her eye makeup and lipstick are perfect. "Okay, right down the middle," she says, but she's not graced with the ability to steer the bed past obstructions. They bump against every pillar, every corner, every elevator door. With each bump Sister Evelyn says "Whoops!", wiggles the bed back and forth, the patient grimaces, and Evelyn says "Hurts, huh? Yeah, I'll bet," and rams on through. It turns out that she's never been in the radiology department, she's only in her second year and this is her first practical experience.

The patient has no idea what the hospital looks like from the outside, but she's gradually getting the impression that it must be a complex of buildings connected to one another by long concrete corridors that seem curiously familiar to her – not a good omen. Anxiously she deciphers the white letters on the illuminated signs that point to WARD B1 or to PHYSIOTHERAPY, once even to RADIOLOGY, but none of that is what they're looking for. Regular working hours seem to be over, they don't meet a single person, Sister Evelyn is already asking herself out loud whether they're ever going to get there, the patient's trying to suppress the panic that's lurking just under the surface of her consciousness when two figures appear in front of them like a vision, young women in colored blouses and swinging summer skirts, chattering and laughing at one another as they walk down the gloomy corridor, virtually bouncing with exuberance, untroubled by fears of any sort, and miraculously they know where the department they're looking for is, politely and precisely they describe the right way. "Well, we've gone off course a little." When Sister Evelyn actually does turn the bed into the corridor indicated by an arrow saying RADIOLOGY, I notice that tears are running down my face for the first time in all those days – how many is it anyway, five? six? – since the local doctor, whom they'd finally called regardless of her objections, made the diagnosis practically before she came through the door: "That's got to be your appendix!" and immediately, again despite her protests, called for an ambulance, which carried her over bumpy roads and into another world. Now she's pretty far down, in every sense. Then she yells out loud. Blinking monstrosities are coming at them, squat, rectangular robots with red signal lights – can you say "on their foreheads"? – that are blinking excitedly as they steer directly at her bed. "Look out!" she screams, and Sister Evelyn says calmly, "Oh, those things!" while at the same time the monsters rumble by right next to them with a humming noise. "What was that?" "Those are just the remote-controlled containers that deliver meals and laundry for us. They're funny looking, but quite practical."

After she's finally been pushed into the room where the gigantic machine is standing, silent and threatening, a super-monster, she still has to get from her bed onto the cradle, another of those impossible demands, there's no one there to help, of course. "Understaffed," someone says. She's the last case of the day. She ruminates on the word "under." A young doctor shows her a cup – she has to drink it quickly. But she can't, she tells him in dismay. He says, "You have to. This is the solution we use as a contrast medium." She puts the cup to her lips. What runs into her mouth tastes more revolting than anything she's ever had to eat or drink. Right down, one gulp after another. She hasn't even put the cup aside when everything she's just drunk, plus all that she'd taken before, gushes back out, soiling her gown, the sheets, the floor – embarrassing, but a relief. Two nurses wipe her off, suddenly there's even a clean gown. She says it's all been for nothing, but the young doctor won't give up, he's going to give the contrast medium by injection. Why not right off? is what she thinks but doesn't say. Why this liquid torture? And provides the answer herself, like a good child: because the injection is probably second best.

Now they're waiting for it to take effect. Now she lets her thoughts roam around fleetingly, urgently, searching for something to hold on to when they push me into the gullet of the narrow cylinder I'm lying in front of, like a loaf of bread into a bake oven. Unfortunately, nothing comforting occurs to me, unfortunately a thought that I've avoided until now comes rushing at me, right here, where I won't be able to shake it off, the thought that Urban has disappeared. Now, at this very moment, I'm no longer able to repress the news that I got on the phone just a short while ago from Renate, his wife, to whom I used to be close, but since we've been avoiding contact with Urban, she's become distant as well. I recognized her voice right away, but didn't understand what she was saying in her frenzied anxiety: "Hannes has disappeared." Hannes? I almost asked, but it occurred to me just in the nick of time that Hannes was the first name of our former friend whom all of us, even Renate, only ever called "Urban." From the level of my fright, I could tell that something bad had happened. "Disappeared? What do you mean disappeared?" "Just what I said, he simply didn't come home." "From where?" "From the institute." "When?" "A week ago." "They're looking for him?" "That's safe to assume. With every means at their disposal." Alarm bells started to ring inside me. She was just letting me know so I wouldn't find out about it in the newspapers. As if that kind of thing got into the papers. Renate had to hang up before she started to cry. I felt my old affection for her reawakening, and toward Urban, something like anger. To do that to her. And a curious feeling of responsibility, as if I had to follow him. Now he's following me, to this very place.

It's not just that your head's the only thing that sticks out of the narrow tube, not just that you couldn't get out, even if you were terrified, even if you were afraid of dying – something that still isn't to be mentioned – it's the realization that you don't even need to have claustrophobia to be afraid when you're in this tube. But I can control it by concentrating on the orders that an impersonal feminine voice is relaying by microphone from the other side of the thick glass pane: "Deep breath – hold your breath – breathe out." A voice that has no idea how hard it can be to follow its simple commands, over and over. I've been at it for ten minutes, because I can see the round clock above the door leading to the dark room behind the glass partition if I incline my head to the left a little, while I have to turn it somewhat more to the right in order to follow the alternating play of greenish lines and data on the screen of the small computer, which, organized and properly interpreted, will give my doctor – who hopefully knows how to read it – valuable information about what's going on in my abdomen. The nausea that's still making me retch is not sensed by the computer, but if we're lucky, said the radiologist beforehand, it will outline the abscess that's causing my fever. "Lucky," he said, and I remained serious. I won't tell him – hardly dare think it – that I'd put up with anything just to get out of this tube. What to do with my arms – they're stretched out over my head with my hands turned so they're starting to go to sleep. "Deep breath, hold your breath, breathe out." I try to fall in with the rhythm, try to sneak in a few breaths on my own, try to conceal my cough so that the impersonal, slightly distorted, technician's voice won't catch me – it can't last more than fifteen more minutes, probably not even that long, that would be out of the question, ridiculous to even think that. "Please try to concentrate." Nothing gets by them.

Calm. Calm down, calm down, calm down. Now I'm pulling myself together. Now I'm breathing quite mechanically, just the way the voice wants me to, and, at the same time, I let the images come on their own. We three, you, Urban, and I, we're coming out of the auditorium after Professor Langhans' lecture. Now I see us – how young we are – as if we were in a photograph from those days, I see Urban's smile, too, you'll point that out to me later. Did you see it? His mocking smile? You'd heard, of course, what I'd said to Urban: "You were really good today," to which he replied, with his "mocking" smile, "You do what you can." And you, as we walked across the bridge over the Saale, in the dark: "But he's just letting on that he's involved. What he's really doing is making fun of it all, haven't you noticed that? – of the text, Professor Langhans, you, all of us." I hadn't noticed it. I didn't want to notice it. "Not just mocking," you said, "diabolical." The word had finally come out, I fought against it, but it burrowed into me all the more strongly. It took years for the word to come up between us again, and, for my part, it took years before I could share with you the insight into Urban's basic problem, his basic deficit, that came to me during his absolutely brilliant interpretation of the text that the rest of us could hardly figure out, Thomas Mann's *A Difficult Hour*. Frau Langhans had picked it for her seminar in rhetoric, a difficult text she admitted, the author describes someone else's crisis, camouflage behind which he half conceals, half reveals his own crisis. Difficult to read. Ambiguous. Urban pulled it off. I kept my eyes on the greenhouses in the Botanical Gardens – where Friedrich Schiller may have walked while he was writing *Wallenstein* and which now lay in view of the windows of our little auditorium – just so no one would notice that tears were forming, not just from empathy with the spiritual and physical torments of Friedrich Schiller but also, and mainly, because of the faint tremor in Urban's voice. Urban, my close friend, my fellow conspirator. Back then I had sharp ears for everthing he said, didn't let myself be put off by the tremolo in his voice when he had to read words like "God-forsaken," "gone astray," or "the holy melancholy of the soul," or the sentence "Pain ... how the word swelled his chest!" No. He was still able to read that sentence with a feigned empathy that might have fooled everyone else, but not you. And not me, either – I who had other reasons for looking at his mouth than you did. He couldn't fool me, not when he was being false, but not when he was being genuine either, when he came across the sentence that seemed to take him by surprise, even more – throw him off balance: "Talent itself ... was that not pain?" The tiny, revealing pause after that sentence, the single, deep breath – those were not put on. Prevented by your prejudice, you hadn't noticed them or couldn't interpret them correctly. But I noticed them and understood them as well, because the question struck me deep inside, as it did Urban, and because, haltingly and not at all confidently, I was beginning to hear a very faint answer, different from his. Because he – that's what I'd grasped – had become aware of the devastating truth that he had no talent, something he longed for more than anything else, and that no power in the world, not even his own burning desire, was going to help him get around that deficit. I felt sorry for him, I felt something almost like a sense of guilt, that's why I looked away from the mocking smile behind which he concealed himself, as always, when we said good-bye in front of the university and that's why, dear, I was so moved. Only later did I learn to fear the vengefulness of ambitious people without talent – and I really learned!

Don't have to breathe anymore. Finally the green, flickering display on the monitor goes off. I couldn't have held out a second longer. An impersonal, male microphone voice calls me by my name. "We're going to take a break now. We've already got the first half behind us." Now all that's needed are detailed views of a certain area of my abdominal cavity that has to be examined more thoroughly. Can I go on? In disbelief, I hear myself saying yes and despise myself for it immediately. For the fact that I can never say no to questions of that sort. The mere thought of keeping my practically dislocated arms over my head for another ten, twenty, thirty minutes! Of being put on display in a cage full of radiation that everyone else has to keep away from. I hear the door open. Steps. A male voice, the radiologist. He's going to put something under my hands to support them. A wave of gratitude floods over me. He's noticed, he comes in, provides some relief. Says they need to define things more exactly. "Something's showing up there. It'll be really valuable information for the surgeon."

So they've already decided on surgery. I breathe the wrong way, then do it again, the young, male voice takes over the microphone, tells me in a paternal tone to just try to be calm. "Concentrate. Breathe in – hold your breath – breathe out." It works, I get the rhythm again, stop thinking. A question hovers in space: What is human happiness? An essay topic from some teacher who wanted us to write that being German was our greatest happiness.

I said that to Urban, in those early days before I knew

you, it's actually true, I knew him before I did you and I must have told him things that later were reserved for you, we were standing in front of the dining hall in those submerged early days, into which I'm being immersed only because of my total helplessness, immersed because I can't summon up any resistance. "Total" is the right word here, normally I can't use it anymore, it's been all used up on the one horrifying question that, depending on your generation, lurks in every sentence in which the word "total" occurs, I hear people saying "total exhaustion," "totally crazy," just today the young student nurse Evelyn said something was "totally unnecessary" – I don't know what, and she might be right, a lot of what people say to her or tell her to do might be completely unnecessary, but the only thing that's total is war. And totally unnecessary as well. What is human happiness today? The question is one I asked Urban in front of the dining hall, he laughed and said, with a faint Saxon accent, parodying the tone reserved for meetings, "Well now really, comrade, the battle against the oppressors!" I laughed. You won't believe it, once upon a time you could have a good laugh with Urban, a word like "diabolical" would never have come into our heads, then Lorchen walked over and announced your presence, I looked up and there you were, standing on the steps in your faded Luftwaffe Auxiliary jacket looking indignantly at Lorchen, then you looked at me, searchingly, and that was some look. The image slid in among the indestructible scenes in my internal archive. "Breathe out, now don't take another breath." Human happiness is everything outside this damned machine, outside of this room with its two tightly closed steel doors.

Lying back in the room that's familiar, almost homey, no matter how many tubes she's hooked up to – there seem to be more and more of them – she's losing her ability to take it all in. If she weren't so weak, it would probably fascinate her to think that you can live without eating and without excreting. That you can lie on your back all day and all night without moving. Suddenly you're there again, standing next to the bed, taking an interest, hiding your dismay over what I have to put up with. No, I say, the real torture's something else. I tell you, with horror in my voice, about the machine lurking in the inner sanctum of this building, the Minotaur in the labyrinth. You're irritated, I can see it in your face, you're in doubt, soon you're going to object to my exaggeration with one of your "but" sentences the way you always do, there, you're saying it already: but now at least they know where they have to operate, that's what the Chefarzt has told you. So you've already talked to him again? You had an appointment with him. Aha.

Tomorrow morning. Comes the dawn, should God wish, you'll awaken again. Among my mother's extraordinary qualities was her beautiful voice. A soprano. Why do you weep, lovely flower girl?

You're not saying a thing.

I'm listening.

It has to be that way.

Who said that? You? The Chefarzt who's also standing by her bed again? So it's tomorrow morning. The two of them are looking at her, expecting her to express something, agreement or protest. But she doesn't want to complain about future things, only about what's already happened. She complains about the liquid. About the huge amount. What a presumption, making her drink that incredible amount after such a long period of nothing by mouth. You can't do that, she says imploringly, defending all those who have yet to experience that same presumption. Yes, says the Chefarzt with his unshakeable politeness. He can see that.

But he once went through tomography himself, to see what it was like ... he stops. She considers it a point in his favor that he stops, cuts himself off. To see what it was like. Puts it in quotation marks as he says it. But it's still not the real thing. Can a leading surgeon, the head of the department, be embarrassed?

She has the little blue book in her hand. It's light, she can hold it in her right hand and use her left hand, the side with the intravenous line, to carefully turn the pages. "Here crowns wend their way in eternal silence / let them reward the industrious / with abundance."

See, I've been looking for that. You say we've had a changeable summer. A sequence of words strings itself together in my brain, changeable flipflop fluttery flowery clichéd clenched painful in pain in the flesh. You ask what you rarely ask because the question is my property, something must have happened to make you ask it now: What do you think? And now – which is really sad – I don't have an answer despite good intentions.

I've always had – you know that – good intentions, frequently the best of intentions, and showed it, eventually all I did was show it because, I can't deny it, gradually my good intentions, put to use too often, got damaged, used up, got away from me. Now, free of good or bad intentions, free of any trace of intent, I can look at you and say no with my eyes. Forget about your question. It's being asked too late. Or too early. Just a little while ago I would still have tried hard to answer it, so as not to offend you, now I'm so powerless that every effort is beyond me. I can't even manage to be amazed that I must have gotten to this point, to the bottom of this mine shaft, so that cares and efforts would pass away. A thought's trying to occur to me, it's as if this entire expensive performance has been put on for no other reason. The idea fades. Pales away. Pallid grove. Ghostly. Owl-like. Dreamlike. I tell you to go. Please go away. Wraithlike. Dreadful. Horrible.

Another flood, a raging torrent, terrifying, forceful, fever-ish, nothing to hold on to. "High," says a female voice, "very high temperature," I drift helplessly in the wild waters, then two words rise up, touch a tiny spot in my consciousness, set themselves against the raging current, hold firm, in amazement I'm able to think: I'm suffering. I move my lips, try to put words to the realization – I'm suffering.

"Yes," says the voice of the Chefarzt dryly, "I know."

That's an important moment. I'm suffering, someone else knows it. No putting on a front for me, no beating around the bush for him. Only the straight truth. "Cold compresses, Sister Christine, if you'd be so kind, try that. If they don't work, an injection."

Only later in the evening, at night, actually – but daytime and nighttime are blending into each other – will the flood waters recede, the room will rise up out of the shadows, barely illuminated by the square night-light in the baseboard beside the door. She will lie, wringing wet and emptied of strength, in her bed-boat, which is rocking but still intact, the two transparent I.V. bottles suspended above her, the pale rectangle of the window half hidden by the curtain, and to the right, on the bedside table, the little black cube, the radio they're reaching for, that they'll turn on hesitatingly, expecting to hear that yet another airplane has fallen out of the sky or an atom-powered submarine has run aground off the northern coast, that in some distant part of the world a hostage has been found dead or someone has been shot try-ing to escape in a nearby part of the world, in other words, that the ways of the world, apparently bearable to every human being but her, have been proceeding normally. Prepared for all that, ready to press the small "off" button immediately, there comes, happily enough, the pure, delicate sound of a violin, followed by another of the same, a fifth higher, then another and another, a bass picks up the first note, a clarinet, her favorite instrument, joins in darkly and resonantly, now they've woven their tones together as finely as a spider's web, now they're giving them an enchanting turn, and at that moment even a trumpet finds its way into that magical land, climbing higher and higher and lifting my heart along with it, all that's missing now is the piano, which has been holding back until the last moment, now it's there, accompanying and unifying the wondrous mixture of sounds. Hey, folks, what's human happiness?

Even her face is wet, a hand wipes it off carefully, carefully her gown is changed, the blanket, the bedclothes. The quiet, nameless night nurse has gotten help, a dark young woman is giving her a hand, she's beautiful, her beauty resides in her light, almost shy, movements. Maidenly, lively, conscientious – the many qualities she's been able to unite in herself are seldom found together. And then she has those deep brown eyes, of a sort I've never seen before. I tell her that. She smiles, without embarrassment. She sits on the edge of my bed, puts her hand on my forehead, maternally, but she's so much younger that she could be my daughter. She's her anesthetist, she says. She'll help her have a good sleep tomorrow morning. She'll be there when she wakes up. She should try to be in a good frame of mind when she goes under anesthesia, because how you go under is how you come out again. She'll be with her and watch carefully, she can depend on that. No, she shouldn't call her "Frau Doktor," she doesn't have that title. Her name is Bachmann, Kora Bachmann. "A name with many associations." She doesn't understand. There's some information she still needs,

I give it to her as well as I can, most of it, she says, is in my records, of course, but she just likes to be sure about things, for instance, whether someone's allergic to an anesthetic agent. She has to reassure herself that the agent will be tolerated by this particular patient. "But," says Kora, "who would want to claim that a poison – which is what every anesthetic agent really is – is tolerated?" Curious. She can even bring up such delicate subjects without triggering my anti-anxiety mechanisms, because how could a drug that Kora is going to inject into me fail to be totally and completely tolerated.

She will lead me into darkness then, into Hades, a feminine Cicerone, she'll watch over me, keep an eye on my heartbeat, I'm reassured. How long these nights are, she adds, and Kora says yes. Her nights are long in a different way, like tonight, when she has the night duty. And then right into the O.R. first thing in the morning, says the patient sympathetically, oh, says Kora, you get used to it, and I'll get a few hours sleep tonight no matter what.

While I'm imagining Kora's night, asking myself jealously whether she's as friendly to other patients to whom she's going to give anesthesia tomorrow as she is to me or whether the same feeling of closeness is developing between them, I fall asleep. I must have heard the sentence "Don't leave me, dark woman" in a dream, probably said it myself, happy and sad at the same time, and then I talked her, Kora, into wandering through the city with me that same night, or to put it more correctly, floating, because we moved with great ease, always a centimeter above the ground. The order that I'd heard so often, "Stay on the carpet now!", wasn't in effect any longer, with ease we floated out of the wide window of our Berlin room and down into the night-darkened courtyard, onto which a single narrow band of light was falling from the sixth floor of the neighboring building to the left, from the kitchen of Frau Baluschek, who really ought to be in bed getting a night's sleep, since she has the municipal housing administration's contract to keep the stairs in the building clean for not much money and on her own initiative knocks herself out trying to keep peace and quiet in our part of the building, which this "mixed public," as she puts it, doesn't always make easy for her, that's the God's truth, especially when she thinks about the new tenants in the front of the building, fourth floor, right, for whose behavior there are no words, or maybe just one word, a single one, which Frau Baluschek never hesitates to come out with: "aaaaa-social." "Those asocials are too lazy to even put their garbage into the cans like any normal person, they have to toss it all around them." Soon the whole courtyard that she's worked so hard to keep looking neat is going to be littered with trash.

"Things aren't running entirely smoothly" is what you said when the yelling back and forth between Frau Baluschek and the new tenants started up over our heads and you closed all the windows, but I wasn't inclined to cross the woman, whom I'd gradually won over with coffee and cigarettes from the Intershop on the ground floor, despite her smoldering distrust of me and thee. But neat or littered courtyards aren't my problem, not tonight, we're floating, the dark woman and I, in the pale light of the moon that's rising over the Friedrichstadt Palace, called "Khomeini's Revenge" because of the design of the façade, down the finally quiet Friedrichstrasse, past the vacant lot on the right hand side that's still there from the war, past Hotel Adria which is degenerating more and more into a gloomy, disreputable-looking barn, then we hover disrespectfully around bronze Brecht on his bench in front of the Berliner

Ensemble. He studies us slyly out of the corner of his eye, pretending that he's dead, a tried-and-true strategy not available to everyone. "Either entirely or not at all," I say to Kora, who agrees with me, a comforting shadow at my side as we approach the Spree.

Standing there, embracing, is a couple. A "young couple" would be wrong, this couple is not all that young, I'd guess they were both in their early or middle thirties. Their clothing, however – that's becoming clearer to me as we get closer – is from an earlier decade, you can tell by their hats. The thirties, I say to Kora. That's what it looks like to her, too. We float across the Weidendamm Bridge behind the couple. At the Prussian eagle, the two of them stop, lean over the cast-iron railing and look down into the Spree. I, right next to the very attractive young woman – she can't see me, curiously that's taken for granted – I look into her face and am shocked, turn to my companion: But that's ... Kora puts a finger to her lips. I'm to be quiet.

I keep quiet. I'm utterly confused because the time periods are becoming hopelessly mixed up. But why hopeless? With the two people whom I believe I know but may not name, because I'd put them in danger if I called them by their names – with those two unnamed people I approach the small park on the far side of the Spree that surrounds the squat building, off limits to the unauthorized, called the Bunker of Tears. I think, Right, of course, that's where they're headed, they're trying to get away, that's suddenly clear to me, trying to get to safety through that exit, lucky it's there, hopefully they have valid visas, hopefully it's not yet midnight or the border crossing will be closed. Then it hits me: what do the two of them want over there? As a Jew the man's in as much danger over there as he is here. Where do they live, anyway, and where do I live, and in what era?

I call out: Kora! But she's gone. I call out: Don't leave me!

"No, no," says a voice. That's neither Kora Bachmann nor Sister Christine. Standing in the middle of my room in filtered morning light is an entirely different human being, who then walks over to my bed and offers me a broad, flabby hand and, mumbling a little, briskly wishes me a good morning while she – yes, it's a female being – pivots on her axis, thoroughly studies every object in my room, including me, nods approval, then comes out with her name before I can ask: "I'm Elvira." She makes a racket pulling the trash bucket from its metal container, takes it out into the corridor to empty it, quickly returns to slide the bucket back into its housing, once again with considerable noise, walks over to my bed again, shakes hands again, saying "So long, good luck!" I see that Elvira's face is deformed, feel the limp pressure of her formless hand, the urge for form has never been able to establish and express itself in her body, but something like sympathy shines through her facial features. I say, "Thank you, Elvira, and bye." "See you later, then, right?" says Elvira. I say, "Yes, see you later."

Sister Christine is angry with herself because she was unable to keep Elvira from bouncing into my room so early. Says she told her to let me sleep, but she's curious, don't you know, there's no stopping her. Sister Christine wants to have a look at the two I.V. bottles herself, wants to check the two drains coming from my abdominal incision and change the flasks in which the fluid accumulates. Then she turns the patient over to Sister Margot, who's a little too fat, comes on a little too loud, and already, this early in the morning, smells of sweat when she bends over her to wash her. She speaks of her – too loudly – in the plural. "We'll soon have all that behind us, can we lift the leg a little higher, what do we think? We want to look our best for the gentlemen in the

41

operating room, don't we?" Finally, she opens the window and leaves, I breathe in the fresh morning air with relief. "So," says Sister Christine, "now for the famous injection. Soon you won't have a care in the world. Just keep thinking, 'This is the last time under the knife.'" All that's left to do now is put the puffy cap on her head, push her hair under it, luckily the hairdresser's just cut it much too short, but unfortunately it's Sister Evelyn again, smartly and perfectly made up this early in the morning, who pushes her bed to the O.R., banging against every corner. We're here a little early, but it doesn't matter. I'm the first one, anyway.

No reason to feel flattered, really, the operating-room schedule isn't made out according to merit and seniority but is based on the severity of the case. She still has time to occupy herself a little with the double meaning of that sentence. Then the O.R. nurse comes in, clad entirely in green, dark sea-green. She introduces herself, "I'm the head O.R. nurse," and starts to talk to her in short, easy sentences. She hears herself answering, from somewhat of a distance, with a few, brief words. She learns, through an increasingly thick layer of cotton wadding, that the nurse is back on duty for the first time today. That she's been out sick for weeks because of the hepatitis she got in the operating room. That she has two children and her husband's a technician. The patient says Oh really? and Yes? and How nice for you, and watches as the nurse, her back toward her, reaches around in the glass case, draws up syringes, no wasted motion.

A man comes in through the door, on which it says OPERATING ROOM 1, and stands there, clothed in the same dark green, with a green cap over his hair, which, as can now be seen clearly, is turning gray at the temples. He wants to say hello before she goes to sleep, it's the head surgeon, he squeezes her hand, looks questioningly at the nurse who says "Everything's in order. I've been talking with her." The patient realizes that it's part of this nurse's job to talk to her, she's not upset. "Good!" says the Chefarzt. "You'll come through it in good shape." She says, "But of course." With a touch of irony, she thinks What else?

The invasion of that little word "good" has reached the operating room. Wasn't good good good the basic chant to which childhood was reduced? "Good?" Urban once yelled at me, "I mean, you're really naïve. Good is the most bourgeois word there ever was. Let man be noble, helpful, and good, absolute bourgeois cant, the catechism of the petit bourgeois who'll work himself up from the word 'good' to 'inhuman' and 'superman.'" But then, still somewhat shy in those days, I replied that that meant he'd long since put that little word "good" behind him. "Like you." "Like we have," I corrected myself. And Urban, tight-lipped, answered, "Watch what you say."

The dark woman, all in sea-green. Like we're all, says the patient, slurring her words slightly, in an aquarium, under water. It might appear that way, says Kora and asks whether everything's okay. Young people's talk. Yes, she says. Everything's okay. Incidentally, I dreamed about you. Oh dear me, says Kora and laughs, though her eyes, brown and gleaming, aren't laughing. The O.R. nurse reports to her, too, while tying her mask behind, that she's talked to the patient. The dark woman nods. "We can go ahead," she says. Suddenly there's another green being there, a man who pushes the stretcher from behind. The two women accompany her alongside, an ordered formation.

The doors of the operating room open. The huge, bright, metal lights on the ceiling. Three men, wrapped all in green, with raised hands. It's a holdup! They're talking about their gardens. "Roses," says one of them, "almost all of the known varieties." That's the Chefarzt, just look, roses! The second says "No inorganic fertilizers!" and the third balks: "A garden? Not on your life." All the while they're holding up their hands as if they're not the perpetrators but the victims, pleading for mercy. The Chefarzt, while continuing to talk about roses, watches closely as the three of them heave her onto the operating table (that's what the orderly said – are we ready to give her the heave-ho?) and have thereby brought her into the zone where she's no longer spoken to, but about. "Is she settled?" "She is." "Can we?" "We can." While the nurse and the orderly restrain her arms and legs, she whispers to the dark woman, now I've forgotten your first name. Kora, she whispers back. Yes, that's what it has to be. Kora whispers, now I'm going to inject something into your left arm. Then you'll go to sleep. Sweet dreams.

Victims of battle human sacrifice depraved criminal

Is it just the first time or the second, third, or fourth time over the following days that, as a well-built, happy, young, blond man, I climb out of the window of our apartment on Friedrichstrasse, which immediately locks behind me, so that with my hair blowing, wearing jeans and a light blue shirt, I'm outside on the narrow ledge that runs around the building, finding little, very little, for my fingers to hold on to as I edge to the left, centimeter by centimeter, toward the balcony of the orthopedist's office, which seems to offer me – me him or me her, apparently unnoticed by a human soul as I hang there above the roaring traffic on Friedrichstrasse – the only imaginable, if somewhat unlikely, possibility of rescue. The picture abruptly fades out. Whoever's calling my name so loudly can't possibly be my rescuer, but he's probably removed my restraints, now he's managing to get me to wake up, of course I hear him, he's practically screaming, now I'm supposed to open my eyelids despite their leaden resistance while he goes on screaming at me even though I hear him. Yes, for God's sake, yes I hear him. Finally I manage to nod my head, which seems to satisfy him. Now I see him. It's one of the three doctors, the one who doesn't want a garden, the tall one, dirty blond, with watery blue eyes. "She's awake. Do we want to wait a little?" "We'll wait a little bit" – a second voice, from the side of the room with the windows. Recovery room, it dawns on me. The zone of the third person. "Wipe her face, if you'd be so kind. Moisten her lips. Is that I.V. going to run out?"

As the young, blond man out there on the ledge, I haven't edged a centimeter closer to the balcony. I either have to go to sleep again, which is what I'd really like to do, or I have to get out of myself. They seem to have decided not to let me go to sleep, even before I've spoken a word, preferably "yes," they're at it. "Are you awake? Let me hear your answer!" But I and the young man out there on the ledge, we know how deeply a word can be buried in a body, what obstacles a sound has to overcome before it can pass the Adam's apple and leave the mouth with the breath. Between hoarse croaks and clearing my throat I get something out that they, who have good intentions, are able to take for a "yes." Yes, yes, of course I'm awake, but I don't want to be, and now they're going to let me go to sleep again. In a flash I'm back out on the ledge, as if it's absolutely my most favorite spot on earth, and there I'm suspended, hanging on for dear life, banished to a beautiful, young, male body, which – if I consider my situation objectively – is condemned to death. "He doesn't have a chance," a voice says to me, and I ask, "Who? Urban?" and hear the voice say, "Who else?" That's Renate. When has she ever talked to me that way? It must have been on the telephone when she said in that flat tone of voice, "They won't find him." I'd said to her, hesitatingly, "Do you

45

want to come over?" We hadn't seen each other for years, odd how you can manage not to cross paths in this small country. She came. The feeling of estrangement remained, it was a tedious conversation, but I learned that after a meeting at his institute during which he'd been sharply criticized, Urban had apparently walked calmly to his car in the parking lot and driven off. One time Renate said, "He didn't have a chance." I understood, but said nothing. In a fragment of a second I'd grasped everything, saw everything in advance, and knew that this was his last chance: to get away, where he couldn't be found. I felt my old affection for her reawaken, and something like anger toward Urban – to do that to her.

Much, much later, after yet another of the operations that were performed on me, Renate told me that her brother, a physician, had said to her, "Your friend doesn't stand a chance," and that she, Renate, had burst into tears and screamed at him, saying if it was really true that only one percent of patients made it through such an infection, that I, her friend, was going to be that one percent. At which her brother shrugged his shoulders slightly. "Whatever you say." For his part, he'd just seen a fifteen-year-old boy die from abscesses that had inexorably spread throughout his belly. That fifteen-year-old boy then became an obsession with me after I heard about him, as if I owed him something, maybe even my life, as if I'd been saved instead of him.

Anticipation of a time in which the word "time" will have meaning again, in which time will pass, or run together, or spread out, in which there will be a time grid, gain of time and loss of time, time segments, points of time, and time intervals, measures of time and determinations of time, half times and decay times, in which there'll be a before and after, days made up of morning and evening, simultaneous times and intervening times, in which I'll cut myself off for a time, then behave like a contemporary again, show up in timely fashion, always come at the proper (or improper) time, in which I'll take time or realize that it's high time, choose the right moment in time, or manage to intervene at the wrong time, feel like a fossil from prehistoric times, believe in the time to come, or just the opposite, consider that the final moment in time has already come.

Right now, nothing counts, neither times of old nor prior times, not when times were good, and certainly not our sober current times, no new times, no probationary time and not the time when it happened. All my temporality has sunk away into timelessness, my time is running away from me like non-time, directly from the operating room she's slipped into a time warp filled with faces and pale twilight, but not subject to any reckoning of time and into which not even the faces that bob up and then disappear, nor the voices she hears, can bring any order. There's no longer any proper time, no failure to appear, there's liberation from the goings-on of time, something that can only be doubted by those who haven't experienced it, who haven't yet dragged themselves forward along a straight timeline with the last bit of their strength. Because holding on tightly on a narrow, very narrow ledge represents an incredible strain, even the impossibility of moving a millimeter costs a great deal of strength. Powerless, indecisive, and without responsibility, I've fallen out of time's net. But even stripped of time, a lot of things can be said – Yes, I'm awake, Yes, I have pain, No, it's not unbearable – but nothing can be narrated without time. I've given up telling, along with knowing, asking, judging, along with claiming, teaching, and understanding, with establishing, concluding, and discovering, with measuring, comparing, and acting. With loving and hating.

But her body hasn't given up learning in that pale parallel world, it's learning unceasingly, without any input from her, learning to lie on its back without moving for days and weeks, learning to keep its arm still when it's connected to the I.V. bottle by the tubing, learning to move its head just a little in order to provide some relief, learning to nourish itself from the fluids that are being infused into its veins. It's teaching itself to hold onto life in this unfavorable situation, while its brain, probably to avoid getting in the way, has closed up shop, switched off, dedicated itself entirely to the body's signals, with one exception – remembering. Or at any rate, a rudimentary form of it. Not that I can tap into my memory at will. But unsummoned and uncontrollable, clumps of memory drift by the sand bar I'm holding on to in this sea of unconsciousness. For example, the light in her hallway as she hangs up the red telephone receiver, Renate's words still in her ear. "Hannes is gone." Midmorning light, falling through the open door of the big room and into the hall. I remember that I thought, "Now they've heard it, too." But then, they know it anyway. And finally, shouldn't I go looking for him? You said no, decisively.

Unceasingly, every single second, a battle must be going on inside me, my body must be taking defensive measures against those attackers that the people in the laboratory have been looking for so feverishly, that the pathologist will call – has already called, but just not to her – "especially malignant." At some point during that unstructured time the head surgeon says, "We think we now know what they are." So there really was some sense to it when the two girls from the lab – one tall and blond, the other short and dark-haired – were poking at her earlobe or fingertip practically every other minute, squeezing out or sucking up a few drops of blood, or when the resident – the one with the black ring of beard around his mouth and chin – drew whole tubes of blood from her arms, which he chidingly and with increasing concern called "barely usable." If only the senior surgeon, the one who won't have a garden, a tall, pale, colorless person whom she's only recently been able to place properly in the hierarchy of physicians and in whom she senses something skeptical, which puts her off, which, really, isn't good for her – if he just hadn't come out with the sentence: "The crucial thing is that they get the medicine to us in time!"

That was an invasion of her place beyond time, of her period of grace, which she didn't like. What did "in time" mean and where did the medication have to be brought in from? All the while, the resident, delighted to explain things, says, "We've got to box them in, you know, those germs!" And the Chefarzt, who, it seems to her, is appearing beside her bed at shorter and shorter intervals, insists that he's quite sure that they've figured out the proper treatment. They're pulling out all the stops.

I have to remember that they don't live on the same earth as I do. That they see me lying there, but don't know – don't even have the slightest idea – where I am in reality. That I'm standing on the opposite shore of that river which has no name and their voices barely carry over to me and my voice certainly doesn't reach them. That I'm getting just the faintest whiff of satisfaction from the moment in which every mask, every disguise falls away and nothing remains but the naked truth, which, of course, is called suffering. That's the way it is. Or that the thought is flitting through my head that perhaps I've been driven to this extreme just because I needed to experience that very thing. Or wanted to. And that "need to" and "want to" have the same root. Now I'm moving in the realm of roots. What I see now is what counts. And soon I will have forgotten it.

Do people talk under anesthesia? she asks Kora, who is sitting on the edge of her bed. Who understands what she means: whether you give yourself away. No, she says, she can't even say for sure whether you dream. We really try to regulate the dose so you're swimming right on the edge, so the anesthesia's not too deep, but certainly not too shallow. I know, I say: floating. She doesn't remember our nocturnal flight, she claims to have hardly ever been in Berlin, certainly never in Friedrichstrasse, she's a real country mouse. She fades, I just barely manage to ask her, perhaps too softly: What is human happiness? At which point, as if it's the key to the riddle, a face rises out of the darkness, young, charming, glowing, but I know that face, don't I, that's the woman who was standing near the Spree with a man and then walked across the Weidendamm Bridge on the night when I floated down Friedrichstrasse with Kora, that's the face of my Aunt Lisbeth as a young woman, fifty years ago, when I was a child. Isn't she dead? And why is she walking over to the neighboring building that was destroyed by a bomb but seems to have rebuilt itself, just like that, in the gap it left behind. I follow my aunt, who climbs the stairs in front of me. Why are these stairs undamaged, well cared-for, covered with a red runner, and the banister, carved wood, gleaming and sparkling when the sun shines through the hall window that still has all of its beautifully colored Art Nouveau panes? So, there hasn't yet been a war. I follow the young woman who was my aunt up three flights to the fourth floor, where she stops in front of a modest physician's nameplate and rings: Dr. Alfons Leitner. A man in a white coat opens the door for her, I watch them as they say hello to each other and as he politely leads the young woman into his office. The doctor has no office help. He invites her to take a seat and tell him the reason for her visit and allows her to talk about a variety of complaints, even about the fact that her doctor, Dr. Levy, happens to be on vacation. Dr. Leitner says he's sometimes seen her walking up and down the street. He must have a lot of time on his hands if he can look up and down Friedrichstrasse from his bay window. He's seen the basic fact – that she's an unhappy woman. Doesn't she know, he then asks her, that she could be letting herself in for some unpleasantness by going to a Jewish doctor, and she, casually, as if sleepwalking, replies that her previous doctor was also a Jew, he just happens to be on vacation. And Dr. Leitner, young, he seems young to me, says with a subtle smile, "He won't be coming back." Lisbeth, however, in her early thirties, simply replies "Oh? Well, then you'll just have to take care of me, won't you, Herr Doktor?" And he, Dr. Leitner, politely: "Is that your wish, madam?" "Yes," says Lisbeth. Yes, that's her wish.

I, however, with that reliably reported scene – that pair of threatened lovers – before my eyes, I have good and bad reasons to break out in a sweat. Nervous sweat, because on the same floor as the Jewish physician, Dr. Leitner, who's no longer permitted to treat Aryans, lives that neighbor lady who's been just waiting for the opportunity to tell him that at that moment a Jew is being shoved down the street with a sign around his neck saying "I am guilty of immoral acts with a German woman." Does he know that? And Dr. Leitner, always polite, replies that he's able to picture it. "Yes, but," I say to him decades later, and he answers, telling me that life no longer seemed very important. Lisbeth, however, my Aunt Lisbeth, threw every caution to the wind. She was so happy, you know. His almost embarrassed smile. Anyway, the neighbor didn't inform on them. And I, bathed in sweat – is it night again already? Did I sleep? Am I sleeping now? – I have to visualize it: Lisbeth on the first floor, Dr.

Leitner in the same building, on the fourth floor. All that up and down the stairs, because she had to take him something to eat, of course, including cake, the way I heard it. I shudder.

Now the Chefarzt puts in one of his frequent appearances, he's coming to let her know that he thinks they've gotten rid of the "focus," at any rate her temperature hasn't gone up too much, she nods in agreement at everything, and says she's not feeling "too bad." The Chefarzt doesn't seem happy with that, but nods and leaves. It occurs to her that she might be able to use Elvira's appearances, which occur only once a day, early in the morning, as markers in this timeless present, but now she can't remember how often she's awakened and seen Elvira whirling around and sending a penetrating gaze toward every object and whether she really did – was it on the very first occasion or later, yesterday or today? – tell about her fiancé, with whom she shares a room at the home and with whom she spends evenings in front of the television after they've had a nice supper together. But she does catch her by surprise each time, by abruptly grabbing her hand and saying, "Well, so long and good luck, okay?"

It gets light only after that, despite the fact that we're headed for the longest day of the year. At any rate, that's what you claim. Apparently all you can talk about is the changeable weather – all those thunderstorms on the way! – and the damage to the farm crops from too little or too much precipitation, after you've once again met with the head surgeon (which I hear about by chance), so it's no wonder the two of you use the same words to describe my condition, and I, addicted to harmony, can't help finding this example of it pleasing. You take up your position at the window, too, and look out, you think the view is beautiful, but it's never even crossed my mind that I could ever walk the few steps to the window and stand there and enjoy the view.

The next time I see Elvira, I'm not sure I'm not being confronted by an apparition that's joining the ranks of the other apparitions in my dream life, which constantly, over and over again, chooses our stairwell for its setting, and even Frau Baluschek, whom you call "unspeakable," is there again, wearing her bilious green beret, demanding that I just look at this example of piggish behavior, I already know she means the large, stinking puddle behind the entry door that she's unfortunately going to have to clean up, something I really and truly don't envy her a bit, although her disinfectant stinks worse than the puddle and although I can't agree with total conviction that it could only be the asocials from the fourth floor who've dealt her such an insult. Carefully, I mention that she might consider that it could also be the drunks from the Adria, who use our vestibule as a urinal because the damaged entry door can't be locked. I don't want to fritter away the good will I've deliberately coaxed out of her with flattery and favors. Cerberus, the hound of hell, I think, but never take her to task when she gets rid of visitors who are on their way up the stairs to see us: "They're not home!" Secretly I thought her incredible gall might have its good side, since it was likely that, among the people that Frau Baluschek sent on their way, there might be several of those strangers who used to ring our doorbell at any time of the day and almost any time of night in order to hand me thick manuscripts or ramble on about problems that often enough were insoluble and just left me depressed, an experience that did not deter me from letting into our hallway two very young people who rang one night, a brother and sister, and listening much too long to the somewhat bizarre, gaunt young man, who had come to yell at me because I'd given too moderate an answer to a letter and a muddle-headed pamphlet that his sister had brought me, instead of calling for action against the state. When at first I answered him in a friendly and understanding way, he went on angrily, haltingly, looking down at the floor with a slightly sour expression and reacting stubbornly, while his young sister looked up at him admiringly. Eventually, having become hostile, sharper, more aggressive, I asked him what, in his opinion, I should have done, taken the lead in some non-existent movement and then gotten the people who wound up in prison as a result – maybe including him and his sister – out again? At which point he insultingly accused me of cowardice, then immediately, almost shocked at himself, begged my pardon. I, however, letting on that I was even more enraged, used the opportunity to get him and his sister – who'd now become pig-headed as well – out the door, a unique event that has pursued me to where I am now, in this shaft, where I still can't find the way out, where it's become so icy cold, however, that suddenly, from one second to the next, she begins to shiver, then shake so hard that the bed rattles and her teeth chatter, so that Sister Evelyn, when the urgent ringing finally causes her to appear in the doorway, is forced to yell "Oh God! Another shaking chill!" and then disappear again, and in her place Sister Christine comes running in, tears the blanket off the empty adjoining bed, throws it over me, and tucks it in firmly, then pushes me down by my shoulders, but I chatter and shake and toss with the chill, which is absolutely the worst one I've experienced here, and, since I can't keep still, the incision hurts worse again as well, there's no more self-control – something dear to me – I can't even control my limbs.

Under ordinary circumstances she would never have allowed herself to carry on that way, so excessively and outrageously, so immodestly and extravagantly, she can't even speak intelligibly anymore, even her organs of speech are overcome by the shaking and chattering, it's even spreading to Sister Christine, who's trying to hold her – she's shaking with her, but apparently it's not a funny sight, because the resident, accompanied by Evelyn, remains completely serious, how long has that been going on, he wants to know. Sister Christine can only vouch for the last ten minutes, and she, the one who's shaking, has no feeling for time, doesn't bother at all about indicators of time, but suddenly, at a speed one wouldn't have credited her with, Sister Evelyn has pushed in an oxygen tank, the physician deftly slips the mask over her face, tells her to breathe, shows her the rhythm, and in fact the chill gradually diminishes, the shaking becomes less violent, Sister Christine can let go of her and stick a thermometer into her mouth, the number, which is absolutely unbelievable, causes the physician – whose name, Knabe, happens to mean "boy" – to remark, "Well that's just great!"

She, however, has now finally relinquished all responsibility, or it's been taken away from her, whatever. If the Chefarzt – all wrapped up in O.R. green, of course – thinks he can confront her and haltingly and carefully prepare her for what's next, he's mistaken. She has to undergo another CAT scan? He really needs reliable information as to whether a new abscess has formed and, if so, where. Why so timid? Just get on with it.

I'm getting horribly worked up. Through my mind flits the idea that someone's out to kill me. I give up that notion, just as I've given up all my outlandish notions lately. Not exactly conducive to work, I think. Someone's grinning within me. I could never reveal such a train of thought to the Chefarzt, after all we're not in a murder mystery here. I wouldn't even burden you with such things. You least of all, dear. What I burden you with nowadays are mostly remarks

55

about the weather, sun-and-rain remarks, because I can see the beautiful, unique cloud formations from my bed, even the way they drop rain across stripes of countryside and just as surely on the lakes as well, you drive by the lakes, don't you, even on a causeway that divides half a lake from the other half and I have no trouble believing that it's a remarkable sight when the right half of the lake is under a rain squall but the left, in contrast, is sparkling in the sun. The colors, you say. Yes, I could visualize them, if I wanted to. Or if I could.

Incidentally, the clanking has started again, the battles and massacres are in full swing again on my internal stage, now I have to tell myself that I wasn't grateful enough, didn't savor things properly when it had stopped. Of course, in my timeless state I have no conception of stopping, but the next time, just in case it does stop again and there is a next time, I'll gratefully relish the peace and quiet. It's clear that those apparitions can't be mentioned to the Chefarzt. When something's clear, once and for all, well, then there's no need to mention important things. Hopefully you've finally gotten that, I say to myself, hopefully you'll draw conclusions from that irrefutable insight, hopefully you won't again forget how to express the ultimate conclusion, or, more important, its meaning. Because there is no "expressing" it, since it consists precisely of avoiding labels, names, words – they're false. Amid the jangling of irons and the wailing of victims, I tell myself that – just in case it occurs to me to use words again anyway, considering how hooked I am on them – so I'll at least know and admit that they're false.

This time he'll be there too, says the Chefarzt, who has shown up again, in white now, and if he thinks that'll be a comfort to me, well, he might be right. And I won't even have to drink anything, he assures me, not even an injection of contrast medium is necessary this time. I nod and nod.

He doesn't really have to excuse himself for what's going on in my abdomen, which they still haven't gotten under control. If I had to, I could tell him a few things about the tricks pulled by my body, which wants to put me out of commission, and I have some inkling – though I still don't know every last detail, don't want to know – about which obligations I'm going to be able to avoid. I allow myself the excuse of thinking that it was getting to be a little too much toward the end. It feels good, malicious thought that it is, but it feels good to have been tossed out of time's net, because on this earth, there's no other way to avoid being indebted to someone for something. The press of time seems to have been shifted to others, Sister Margot seems to be under time pressure now, quickly, quickly, she again changes my gown that's been soaked through yet again, "I mean, really," she says, "there can hardly be any fluid left in you," quickly, quickly, but deftly, she pushes my bed through the corridors and elevator doors, she knows the way, doesn't allow herself to be intimidated by the blinking, orange computerized monsters that are wandering aimlessly around the underworld again, in a firm tone she says "Now behave yourselves!" and they come to a halt.

And she hasn't forgotten my chart, either, it's lying at the foot of the bed. Sister Margot's on the ball, she even helps lift me onto the cradle in which they'll immediately slide me, with my arms extended over my head, into the narrow cylindrical scanner. The Chefarzt is there, he's kept his word, once again he explains to me what they're going to do now, another physician is standing next to him, he has graying, carefully trimmed hair, he's wearing a lead apron, he's introduced to me, offers me his hand as if we're at a party, he's a department head as well, of radiology in fact, and he's going to stay with me.

Well, that's a bit of good news. Now they won't hear a peep from me, I'll be a good little girl and follow the orders that come from the other side of the glass shield, it even seems to be the same young woman's voice that's going to tell me when to breathe and when to hold my breath. The radiation exposure with this device is supposed to be much less than with the usual x-ray apparatus, it's really very low dose radiation, otherwise it would be out of the question for the physician to stay in the room, no matter how much lead's protecting him, or for him to even take my hands as they search for something to hold on to at the other end of the tube, then get a leather bolster that I can rest them on. "Better?" Much, much better. Now my shoulders aren't being dislocated, now it's almost a pleasure to breathe, then stop breathing.

I really believe I'm doing it just right, once you learn it, you don't lose it, I mean earlier, when I was young, because she must have been young once, of course, her body was exposed to radiation, at short intervals at first, then at longer and longer ones, "follow-up" they called it. I can see the building in front of me where those checkups took place, a dilapidated old structure with cracked stucco on the outside, and inside, stone staircases, dirty paint on the walls, worn linoleum. A sliding window in the wooden partition across the waiting room, behind which my file was looked up after my name was called out, always huge rooms, divided into different areas by partitions, an area to wait, an area to change, then the room in which the machines were located, antiquated old things against whose cold plates she had to press her chest, breathe, hold her breath, breathe normally. Always an element of fear. Residual fear, they'd say nowadays, and an irrational degree of relief when she was standing outside again, knowing they hadn't found anything.

Hadn't she run across Renate one day, after one of those follow-up sessions? She seemed distraught, I now recall, out of habit she asked how I was doing, she wasn't really interested, we walked down a long, ugly street with potholes and a sidewalk in need of repair, toward the university, I began to question her carefully, until, hesitatingly, as if she needed to beg my pardon, she came out with it: now she and Urban were "really together." I had to smile, it had been a topic of conversation in our group for a long time, so why did she have such an unhappy expression? "Unhappy?" she asked, taken aback, now looking not only unhappy but guilty as well. She wasn't striking looking but was charming nonetheless, didn't see anything charming about herself and couldn't figure out why Urban, who could have had almost any girl, made a play for her in his strange way, namely, by criticizing her more frequently than previously, even more frequently than he criticized the rest of us, so that she – insecure as she was anyway – nearly perished from insecurity. He, on the other hand, when I took him to task after she'd run out of one of our section meetings almost in tears, with his head politely inclined forward, asked how so, was he to understand he hadn't behaved fairly toward Renate? Did I perhaps think she'd been unjustly treated? Or that the private and political spheres could be separated from one another? I didn't think so. I couldn't find words for my discomfort. Urban, you see, had considered it necessary to report that Renate had recently revealed something to him in a private conversation: that she was still attached to her homeland, Silesia, although she of course recognized the Oder-Neisse line. Her feelings were just limping along behind her understanding, that's not a crime, said Urban, but it certainly wasn't being nasty to Renate to tell her she had to work on herself. Renate didn't say a thing and when asked whether she was in agreement with that assessment, she nodded, though she was quite pale. She was the first to leave. I think I recall telling Urban, "You need to smooth things over with Renate." "Oh, of course!" he said cheerfully. "Point of honor!"

"Hello, hello, we've lost the rhythm!" She's noticed that herself. She breathed the wrong way. "Doesn't matter," says the doctor with the lead apron and touches her hands again. "In a few minutes we'll take a break anyway, we've gotten pretty far." Only to the break? That just can't be true. She breathes the wrong way again, and then again, the voice of the young woman on the other side of the glass shield is getting impatient. "Once more!" she says. "Rrr . . . ight now!" Things are going properly now, heading for the break, they've pulled her out of the tube for a bit, let her move her arms, told her about how much longer it will take – that long again, which was hard to imagine, of course, but people can endure more than they think, that's what my grandmother said and endured more than I would have.

Of course – if I ever wanted to talk about Urban's early days – I'd have to be very careful not to expose him to any tacky urge to condemn. "Ha, we've got you, you scoundrel!" We don't have him – that sentence now has a distressing double meaning. We never had him completely, he slipped away from our judgment over and over again, but he must have really gotten his hooks into Renate, he never let go of her, she still didn't know exactly what she wanted or whether she even wanted anything at all, from him or with him, then all of a sudden she'd already said yes. "I don't know, myself, how it happened," she said to me, we were at Brühl's, there were furs on display for the first time, we were standing in front of the show windows, staring in, they could just as easily have put the moon in the show window as an expensive fur coat. "But you do love him, don't you?" I said awkwardly. "I really don't know," said Renate, looking as if she were at the end of her wits. You have to give Urban credit for having chosen this plain yet sensitive and loyal girl, who was incapable of hurting a single person.

"Yes," says the doctor in the lead apron – now that he's standing close beside her head, she can see that he's no longer young, his steel-gray hair is cut like a close-fitting cap that makes him look younger, he's suntanned, it must actually be summer outside, she can easily imagine him in a sailboat on one of the many lakes. Two deep but not unbecoming folds run from the sides of his nose to the corners of his mouth – "Yes," he says. "That's it for today." He helps get her over onto her bed, says goodbye, even bows – party's over. Then he adds, "Things are really not going very well for you right now, but it doesn't have to stay that way. There are treatments for it and we'll find the right one."

Those are not sentences she wants to hear or can tolerate, how is it that he doesn't know that? What does "not very well" mean, what does he mean by "doesn't have to stay that way"? "They talk a lot when the day drags on," says Sister Margot, but she's not the one who has the discomfort in her abdomen, and it's going away only very slowly, even the little radio doesn't contribute much, it's not yet time for classical music. Late in the afternoon, when your temperature goes up if you're sick, all the stations are broadcasting what they call "information," which she fears like the plague and turns off immediately, even before the first few sentences – which are already horrible enough – are out. So, for the moment, she doesn't hear where the ferry went down, doesn't learn the number of flood victims, they even think she's up to picturing Vienna, where negotiations about nuclear warheads are underway, but she can't, all the cities in which negotiations about insane topics are taking place, or where there's some "summit" meeting or other, turn into the most abstract places on earth for her, at any rate, not places where people can simultaneously ride around in horse-drawn carriages. Nor does she want to know how high her temperature is, she doesn't ask and doesn't protest when Sister Margot comes in with an injection to "knock it down," even though they both know it will nauseate her. And she can't possibly get any weaker, this constant dripping of "liquid nutrition" into her veins has to have some effect. Didn't the Chefarzt promise to "build her up" and isn't it possible that the building-up is going on in her cells right now, but she just doesn't notice it?

"Build up, build up." Do you know the song? I ask the dark woman, who – incidentally, I don't know in which of the various realities where I spend time, on my internal stage or in the external world – is sitting on the edge of my bed again and, like all physicians, is trying to conceal her worried expression, an art which she doesn't command as well as my Chefarzt or even the tall, pale senior surgeon, who, of all my doctors, is the most impenetrable and impersonal. No, Kora doesn't know the building-up song anymore, it doesn't even interest her, she feels my forehead, takes my pulse and says "Here we go again," but I still don't know, of course, that she's going to put me to sleep again the following morning, she's shocked to hear that, now she's the one who has to tell me, but I'm not to let on to the Chefarzt that I already know, it's his place to give me the news, apparently he's been delayed somewhere. I ask her why there has to be this whole chief, senior, and junior business with the doctors, anyway, she laughs a little, amused. But I can't resist approaching her with the question that's been bothering me: whether everything that's been going on with me might not be thought of as punishment. Then she gets angry. "For what?" she yells indignantly. "What can you be thinking of?" yells Kora, so loudly that it echoes on my internal stage. Yes, what can I be thinking of, anyway?

And what can the Chefarzt be thinking of when he obviously takes such trouble to pick the least worrisome words to tell her that he's going to have to operate on her again, the results of the CAT scan have made that clear, but now he knows exactly where the abscess is located and also knows how to get at it, he can put the computer image up in the operating room and use it as a guide, says it's really quite a luxury – that's the sort of word that occurs to him. She says yes, yes, each time, yes. He's sorry, puts on his poker-face, but as he's leaving, he places his hand on hers briefly and presses it gently, that could bring tears to her eyes. Or, as Sister Margot expresses it, "start the whole mess all over again."

Finally a word occurs to me that gets to the heart of the matter: poisoning. I'm poisoned, I think, what I need is a detoxification, purification, purgation. Quite a discovery. That it's come so late remains a matter of surprise. And that it's so stressful. More of a stress than the poisoning itself. The infection may have occurred at an early age, the decade-long incubation period is over, and now recovery is breaking out in the form of severe illness. All that remains is to name it. "Named, tamed." Where did I hear that?

The night following the injection is awful, the nausea comes over her again, every few minutes someone checks on her. Sometime or other she falls asleep. "All reason's dashed!" is announced to her threateningly and with finality in the middle of the night, there's actually a character who speaks such sentences. But all the rest of it she knows already – Elvira, the scraping of trash buckets, her limp handshake, the bathing procedure that stresses her to the limit, Sister Christine with the O.R. cap and the sedative injection. "Okay," she says, "we'll do them the favor one last time, but then let's not go through this drill again, that would be even better." Her curly blond hair makes a pretty frame for her face. She pushes the patient to the O.R. herself, there's another nurse waiting in the prep room, Sister Nadeshda, who tries to talk to her, too, but haltingly, her German is far from perfect, says she's from Leningrad, marriage brought her here, an engineer. She turns her back to her and draws up injections, the patient says "Nadeshda" means hope, the nurse seems happy that she knows that.

The Chefarzt comes in to tell her he'll approach the abscess from the side this time, so there'll be a second incision. She finds the man very conscientious, Kora Bachmann gives a little laugh behind her mask when she tells her that, lisping slightly, her tongue isn't as nimble as usual. "You're the only person I ever see laughing," she says to Kora, who immediately becomes serious. The three doctors in green are standing silently next to the O.R. table with their hands up. "Reception committee," she says jestingly. She doesn't manage to get a laugh from anyone today. "We can go ahead," says the senior surgeon.

There's no falling away into darkness. Unconsciousness does not overwhelm me gradually. There's no transition. There's only being here and no longer being here. "What goes on there?" I ask Kora. "What's taking place while I'm gone?" She says, "We don't know. We really don't know. We separate the brain from the body, we prevent the brain from registering the sensations that are sent to it. More than that we don't know." "And the risk?" I ask her. She doesn't answer. The senior surgeon says, "There's basically always a risk." The Chefarzt, unwillingly: "Minimal." He seems to know most accurately what I want to hear. "Is it the same with dying?" I ask. Now the head surgeon, too, has to say, "We don't know." "To which brain are the connections cut?" I ask Kora. "To the higher, mammalian part of the brain certainly, probably not to the reptilian brain." So that it would be perfectly possible that it could go on sensing those stimuli unhindered and transferring them to the respective regions of my body. "To take me just as an example," I say to Kora, who has the night duty again and apparently isn't terribly busy, "I experience myself, in other words, as a reptile, of course without carrying the least bit of that experience over into my conscious life, but who really knows? Could that be the reason why I often see myself as a dinosaur?"

Kora smiles again, it's never a superior smile, she hasn't turned on a light, there's only a dull glow from the squarish night-light in the baseboard. The window curtain is pulled halfway, shadowy clouds drift past an almost round moon. "'You again fill forest and valley.' Do you know that?" I ask Kora. She says, "I didn't learn a single poem in school, we had a revolting teacher." It occurs to me that I've never imagined Kora without a poem. I'll have to rethink her. For the entire time, once again, she's put her hand on my body in places where it feels good, she's blotted my face with a lukewarm, moist cloth, she's rolled a blanket together and put it under my heels. "They must be hurting by now." They've been hurting for days, but I thought that's how it was supposed to be. Kora can sit there calmly, leaving her hand on my upper arm, I imagine she's smiling again, and say sleepily, "But you could be my daughter," and she says, "Why 'but'?" and then her pager beeps, she answers quietly and says she'll come right away, and tells me she has to go. I'll have a restful night.

Kora, the night and moon woman who watches over my

sleep should know the hymn to the moon. Now finally giveth / my soul release. "Release," "relieve," "dissolve," words in which there are magical powers, carry me over and down. Into the depths. Into the shaft. And so he journeys with his light by night / down into the mine. My body as a mine. The miner's lamp that lights the way. That casts a faint beam, microscopically small, that enlarges every cell in my body to a cave, every artery to a riverbed, and the blood to a stream that progresses with each pulse down a widely branching network, along which the light penetrates deeper and deeper. Feels its way over organs, bizarre mountain formations, swampy fields, pipelines that stand for nothing other than themselves. This joy in the factual, after so many years over-loaded with significance, left in shreds by pronouncements and counter-pronouncements. I let myself drift, but is it still "I" that's letting itself drift? The light of consciousness that's tolerated in here, down here, only as long as it doesn't cause a disturbance, carries me along, through barriers, nets, past obstacles, slight movement, a swimming and gliding in the realm of the scarcely even physical, shadowy goings-on that are visible yet defy description, but which still convey to me the shocking insight that there is a realm, or whatever I should call it, in which the differences between the spiritual and the physical disappear, in which one affects the other, one proceeds from the other. One is the other. Therefore there's just one. So that would be the locus of the essential – would it be worthwhile to learn that?

Suddenly, we're – am I to assume I'm no longer alone? – at the place of the confrontation, on the battlefield, in the thick of it. The sight is a shock. If that's what's going on . . . who's to hold back those virulent masses? As far as the eye can see, throngs of destructive cells hurling themselves upon the healthy tissues. But that's not allowed. Things aren't supposed to happen that way. Something's got to be done. I – the "I" that's followed me here – decide to intervene and collect my forces. I reassure myself that they're with me and hurrying up from all sides. I'm in command. I think as forcefully as I can: Annihilate them! My forces obey. Before my very eyes the antibodies hurl themselves bravely into the fray and annihilate whole armies of those revolting things, even pursuing them as they retreat. That's the way. Keep at it. But it's tiring. There's nothing more we can do for today. I pull on the line. Rising up, consciousness takes on significance again and forgets the scenes in the depths.

"Yes," says the doctor on night duty, "the incisional pain, I can believe it. You can certainly have another injection, it's ordered for you." She doesn't want one. She doesn't want to have the connections between the individual parts of her threefold brain severed again. Says there's still some effect from the anesthesia. "As you wish," says the night doctor. At her request he pulls the curtain back. In the middle of the large window, the moon stands against the clear sky. Yet I once possessed / that which is so precious. If she could, she'd laugh at how precisely another person had expressed her sentiments two hundred years previously. And, I once asked you, what are we going to do when that which is precious is gone, once and for all? You don't like questions like that. What does that mean, "once and for all"? What did I want to know that for? And besides, you just can't simply give up in midstream because things aren't precious any longer. Why not, I thought, but didn't say it. Really, why not? And now, to my torment / never can forget. Now I can – and I'm thankful for it – hold onto the word "torment" and don't have to come out with it myself.

Sometimes Urban held us up as hopeless romantics, Renate and me, said we simply couldn't keep ourselves from idealizing authors. Instead of striving for objectivity. We got ourselves tied up in endless discussions with him, do you remember, you were the only one who could put on an indifferent expression and shrug your shoulders. Kleist? He's supposed to be a forerunner of irrationalism? Didn't the bunch of you notice that Urban didn't have a clue about literature? That's the whole point. But it wasn't "the whole point." At least, it was a long way from being the whole point as far as our friend Urban was concerned. And he indeed did have a clue about literature. Do you still recall what the professor we all admired said to him once? "Sometimes, dear Urban, one might think you love literature." And do you remember how embarrassed he got?

No sleep. I have to try not to think certain thoughts at night. Before it gets light, a curious thing occurs to me: shortly before the age at which – so I imagine – reality begins to pale, I've succeeded once again in experiencing something real. Something, moreover, that's quite implausible. That I'd better not believe, that would be really dangerous to believe. But that's the way it is with reality in general – I think to myself in the lucid, nearly fever-free hour that's granted to me between three and four in the morning – it's most concentrated just when we can't believe it at all. In the early morning comes an hour of sleep, and with it a dream: my mother sitting on her mother's lap, frozen in a block of ice, my father bending over them, vainly trying to pry them loose. I, a child, on my father's back.

When she awakes, she's cold.

Elvira's standing in front of her, shakes her hand, turns, surveys the entire room, then the trash bucket clatters. Today she tells her what kinds of sausage there are for supper at her home and that her fiancé loves mettwurst but she loves liverwurst, so they can always trade sandwiches, a glow of happiness flits across her face, a reflection from it strikes me. Liverwurst sandwiches come to mind, the ones I made toward the end of the war, at the age of fifteen, in the gymnasium of the Hermann Göring School, for the refugees from West Prussia who were seeking shelter in our town, which hadn't yet been evacuated by the inhabitants. I wonder whether the longing for security and the realization that there's no such thing have been fighting violently within me ever since.

Then come other figures who get to work on her: inspect the drains, change the I.V. bottles, wash and reposition the thing my body is for them. Nothing I would ever have wished for myself, but could I ask them to stop immediately? I can't. From which it can be inferred that wishes use more energy than declarative sentences, energy that I don't have.

The number of diagnoses that I can't mention to the Chefarzt is growing. I hope he's concealing less from me than I am from him. But he surprises me. He asks, while looking at me searchingly, as if he's actually expecting an answer, "Why is your immune system so weak?"

Just tosses the question at me, my Chefarzt. Doesn't he know that it's a mouthful that I have to chew over? Does he think I'm that much recovered already? Can't he think of a way to shock me anymore, other than with such questions?

Already in his green gown and green cap, he asks Sister Christine to quickly tell him about my temperature, I sense – don't see, he knows how to control himself – that he's not happy with the figure, not entirely happy, he'd never raise his eyebrows in reaction to it the way the resident, Dr. Knabe, will later, the Chefarzt simply says, "We can tolerate that, considering that she's just post-op." "Still tolerate that," Dr. Knabe will say and lower his eyebrows again. No one mentions my immune mechanisms again, but the problem is that my temperature climbs over the course of the day, and apparently they neither can nor will accept that. Even if it were a reaction to the operation, it would still be too violent a one, hence still not healthy, not normal, but rather a sign – of what, they don't say. Even the tall, colorless senior surgeon, who apparently is on duty in the afternoon after the others have left, is stingy with his words.

Of course you're here again already, of course you've spoken with the Chefarzt the way you do every day around noon, but even he seems to be stingy with his words. My temperature has to come down, even I'm aware of that, but I don't want another injection, I get nauseated after them. I want cold compresses, like when I was a child. The Chefarzt, who also shows up again even though he can't possibly still be on duty, says "Why not?" He'd had that injection once and even he'd tolerated it poorly, so he understands. He's now saying words with feeling, like "understand." "Well, then, Sister Thea, if you'd take care of that . . . if you'd be so kind."

Sister Thea nods, she's new to me, just back from vacation today. Small, inconspicuous. The Chefarzt is amazed, I'm amazed, too, that everything he needs in order to examine and re-dress my abdominal incisions is right there, ready for him, that's something that's hardly ever happened before. Even the plastic gloves are there, in his size, several pairs, since he regularly tears one or two pairs while putting them on, the quality is something over which they have no influence. The Chefarzt doesn't curse, he never does that, today he doesn't even allow himself a remark, doesn't scowl, throws the torn gloves in the basin that Sister Thea has ready as well, deftly she opens a new pack for him, the third pair remains intact. Sister Thea has already exposed my incisions, she knows how much fluid has come out through the drains, can describe the character of the fluid, anticipates what the Chefarzt will need next, forceps, gauze, disinfectant, the non-allergic tape – do we still have some of that? We do. Sister Thea has already cut the tape strips to the right length, pulls them off the edge of the bedside table, I hardly notice it as she tapes the gauze down across the incisions, she's already taken off my old gown – "soaking wet!" – and is already slipping a new one on. The Chefarzt has been watching her silently. "I thank you very much, Sister Thea," he says, and leaves.

Then the two of you – Sister Thea and you – start on the cold compresses. The first ones evaporate – I take it that she considers that entirely normal. It requires patience, they need to be changed frequently, you take over. Even Sister Thea prefers this natural treatment to the endless injections, that encourages us. Aren't the intervals between compresses gradually becoming longer? Maybe it only seems that way to me, I have no sense of time, I let myself go, float away, but hear what you tell me as you're putting another set of cold towels around my calves: Today's June 27, St. Swithin's Day, and it has rained heavily. So it'll be a wet summer. They've already had problems with the grain crop. Too damp, everything. Too little sun. "And then there are those constant thunderstorms," says Sister Thea, who lives in a village nearby, still with her parents in fact, but at least she doesn't have to share a room with her brother, who's with the army right now. She puts her hand on my forehead. "Well," she says, "now I think we can . . ." Takes my temperature. "There we are. We'll settle for that. Not exactly spectacular, but it is down." No objections.

Kora, who just wants to look in again – officially she doesn't have anything more to do with her today, thanks be to God – also considers it "passable," but also thinks they should keep at it. "Your husband can go home now," she

suggests. She'll take over a bit for him. No, he can't sleep
with his wife, he'll have to be patient for a while. Kora teas-
ing, that doesn't fit her. "Tomorrow the world will look different again. For today, I believe we've gotten it under
control." You don't believe her, you never were able to hide
your feelings. What would it accomplish if you voluntarily
spent the night in the hospital? Hey, I say, none of that stuff.
That's a secret code between us. No, no, you say, but your
expression doesn't brighten up.

When you've gone, when Kora and Sister Thea have
stopped changing the compresses, I'm tempted to turn on
the radio for some diversion. A few bars of music that are
worth hearing, Vivaldi I'm informed, but they're already
shifting over to the news and I can't operate the "off" button quickly enough because I have to do everything while
lying on my back, so I'm forced to listen as they report that
a dead infant has been found in the basement of a building
in Berlin, murdered by his twelve-year-old brother, it turns
out. Panic rises within me. How can I deal with a dead infant?
It's already swimming, like a fetus in a specimen bottle,
etched on my retina, it takes a while for me to recognize that
image again, I've already run away, blindly, at first it seems
to me I'm submerged again in the arterial network within
me, swimming, then letting myself drift with the current
when I can't fight it, without any help from me it washes me
up on the battlefield again, which I scarcely recognize
because it's so changed – for the worse, I have to confess –
the sick and the healthy can no longer be distinguished, my
attempt to influence things accomplishes nothing, something inside me knows what that means, I'm already somewhere else, wading, the water or whatever it is – blood? – up
to my knees, at every fork choosing the alternative that leads
me further down into the darkness. Those aren't even arter-

ies any longer, I'm plunging down into even deeper darkness, the fetus constantly in front of my eyes, glowing in its
retort glass – the homunculus? – and in addition, growing.

The stairs are already behind me, someone must have
given me a key to the cellar – Frau Baluschek? Unlikely, she's
stingy with her cellar keys: What do you want down there,
are you trying to tell me you have coal there? There's a gas
heater on the outside wall, anyone can see that. Well, okay.
So I'd probably have gone to the ladies for the key, two
cousins who've started to call their little drugstore right next
door to our building "the boutique," who, in difficult negotiations with the municipal authorities, managed to obtain
permission to switch their inventory from soap, toothpaste,
and toilet paper to deodorant pads, candlesticks, and per-
fume. They, of course, have a storeroom in the cellar, happily give me the key, this time even closing their shop ten,
fifteen minutes ahead of time, so we won't be disturbed by
customers while they're telling me all about the colleague
from the Postal Service who requests the key to the cellar at
irregular intervals, just as I do, but of course for different
reasons – ostensibly to once again repair faulty phone connections in the junction box in the basement. The two ladies,
however, the Keepers of the Keys to the Underworld, know
as well as everyone in the building that there are no defec-
tive phone connections – unless yours is not working? Well,
there you are. They said that right to the face of the reserved
but by no means impolite colleague, who despite, or perhaps just because of, his brand-new neat-as-a-pin uniform
was certainly no phone repairman from the German Postal
Service, and they claim to have even asked him – because
what did they have to lose? nothing – if he had to change
our tape-recorder cassettes again. "Tape recorder" was the
cousins' imaginative term for that little, pale green, sealed

metal box in one of the front rooms of the basement, into which – we'd convinced ourselves – only a single line fed, regrettably enough the one from our telephone, and from which, of course, just the one line led away, only to – casually, feigning innocence – join up, a few meters further, with the fat cable coming from the other telephones in the building, which ended in the large junction box that was accessible to everyone. We didn't believe for a moment that it was a "tape recorder" that was concealed in the little metal box, but we found it useful to have the boutique ladies – one was light blond, the other jet black, both middle-aged, still quite presentable – give us reliable reports about the visits of the repairmen, thus providing us with topics of conversation, up to and including the question of whether they always made a point of politely requesting the key from the ladies just so that they, in turn, would tell us. That modus operandi had been heard of before.

But, since I'm down here, I have to push on further than ever before into the tangle of cellar corridors, I must have been in the company of the boutique ladies, must have been made aware, regrettably, that soon they were going to suspend sales of that bath oil, which – though it was considered a scarce commodity – I'd previously been able to obtain regularly from them. I'd said that I had a hard time imagining my daily shower without that oil, whereupon the black-haired one had asked her blond cousin in a conspiratorial tone, "What do you think, Marlies, shall we?" And Marlies allowed her eyelids to fall in agreement: Jeanette should. Five bottles of Yvette's Camellia Bath Oil must have been wrapped up just for me and stowed away in a plastic bag on which, in tasteful lettering against a gold background, were the words "Boutique Jeanette" and which – I remember exactly – I was carrying at first. I must have lost it somewhere or set it down as I made my way into the next dark cellar room, feeling my way along with my toe.

The light bulbs must have burned out here a long time ago, no one, not even the telephone repair man, ever wanders in here, so for years no one's needed light. But of course, the retort with the homunculus is flying – or what should I call its form of movement? gliding? – ahead of me, turning corners that I don't see, enticing me on into rooms in which, sometimes, a rickety light switch still works and a dust-coated bulb that probably entered service during the war or in the early postwar years emits a dim, fluctuating light. The laborious reconstruction projects in the upper parts of the building complex, stretching over several months, never penetrated into the subterranean zone. There were, as the construction supervisor confided to me, no blueprints, no plans, not even any individuals with knowledge of the extended, subterranean labyrinth to which our cellar system doubtless was connected. "If anyone gets lost in there" – our construction supervisor speaking again, a somewhat hesitant Mecklenburger with an aversion to anything that smacks of the big city – "God help him."

It turns out that every room leads to further rooms in which I've never set foot, back in one corner there's a lattice door that's hard for me to open because it scrapes along the ground, but I have to, even if I'm timid about it, because I have to find the cellar where the infant was murdered. The cellars are stacked together according to some indecipherable pattern, now I'm wading through dust and piles of ancient trash in the corners, suddenly there's a rat in front of my feet, fleeing at a leisurely pace. Now I notice for the first time that the glowing retort with the homunculus has disappeared, there's no longer anything to show me the way, I've lost my bearings long ago, all I know is that I have to search for the murdered infant, although I have an un-speakable horror of it. Eventually there comes a time when you have to pursue what's forgotten. I'm wandering around in the burial labyrinth of children never brought into the world, I'm forced to dwell on the meaning of the phrase "never brought into the world" while I walk, stumble, and feel my way forward, now there aren't even any of the dim light bulbs anymore, I now have in my hand a flash-light that casts a weak beam, somebody must really want me to keep on going and has supplied me with this essen-tial item.

At the moment I'm following arrows on the wall, previ-ously white but now almost totally faded, beneath which are words that will never be forgotten by anyone who once knew them: AIR-RAID SHELTER. For a brief moment, I'm amazed that the shelter would be located in this cellar labyrinth so far away from our building, because our build-ing remained standing, nearly undamaged, while the neigh-boring building was hit by a blockbuster during one of the last air raids and totally destroyed, and, for the first time, I'm forced to ask myself whether the people in the neigh-boring building were really all killed back then or whether some of them were saved – perhaps by being able to work their way from the far side to the spot where I'm now stand-ing and deciphering the faded letters: WALL BROKEN THROUGH. A reflex, frightened: Which wall? But this wall, here, was broken through a long time ago, I can get through the gap by bending over and climbing over loose debris, and find myself in a room that almost totally resembles the one from which I've come – no, is identical to it – and the next one is identical to the last one behind me, I recognize it again from the remnants of wooden shelving on what was previously the right-hand wall but now is on the left, with

dust-covered, dirty mason jars on which I can barely make
out the labels once written by a German *hausfrau* in neat,
old-fashioned Sütterlin script: "Cherries 1940," "Rabbit
Stew 1942." I try to imagine where that woman got a rabbit
in 1942, in the middle of the war, maybe her parents had a
victory garden, but what's really bothering me is the suspi-
cion, then the certainty, that after passing through the hole
in the wall, I've wandered into an area that's an exact mirror image of the one I was moving around in before I came
to the breach. There are the arrows on the walls, now pointing in the opposite direction, there's the trash in the corners, finally the rickety light switch, familiar in an uncanny
way, and the rat that slinks away. What does all this mean,
am I to be led through ever newer halls of mirrors? I feel
myself walking faster, breathing more rapidly, I want to get
out of here, then the homunculus bobs up again in his retort
glass, giving off a bluish light, it's too much.

Then the woman walks over, young, charming, full of
life, she snatches the homunculus, who's now grown into an
infant, out of the air, takes him in her arms, I recognize her
and call "Lisbeth!" But I'm not seen, not heard. Invisible,
the magic cape, often wished for. The woman flees now, in
panic, I'm right behind her, want to calm her, rescue her,
then the man walks over to her, not tall, delicately built. He
embraces her, caresses her, comforts her, he takes the child
who, it appears, will not be murdered, will be permitted to
live, now the three of them are walking together in front of
me, we find our way into those poorly lighted cellar rooms
that I already know, then comes the big cellar that's divided
into sections for the various tenants. Through the gaps in
the latticework partitions, I see old-fashioned bicycles, heaps
of briquettes, neatly stacked firewood, junk, piles of newspapers, I read the *Völkischer Beobachter*, as if in a dream I

walk on, painlessly immersed in the year 1936, a sleepwalker in the cellar rooms of the neighboring building that was destroyed by bombs forty-four years ago, in 1944, following the family of Aunt Lisbeth, which, as I well know, is not a family and, under threat of extinction, will never be permitted to be one. I sneak up the cellar stairs with them, unnoticed, and with the boutique ladies' key unlock the cellar door, behind which – not much can astonish me now – stands the plastic bag with my bath oil. I follow Lisbeth, who's calmed down and is carrying her child tenderly, up to the second floor and over to the door on which stands her husband's name, which is also her name and that of her little son, in front of which she stops, takes the key from her apron pocket, and her companion, the father of her child, who has to part company from her there, embraces her, after having first looked carefully around the stairwell. I was worried by the thought that he could see me, the seven-year-old child, worried by the question of what that child would have made of the fact that her aunt had had a child out of wedlock by a Jew. He doesn't see me, and so, invisible, with heavy and oppressed heart, I follow the man, who, bent over, slowly climbs two more flights in a building that hasn't existed for a long time, up to the door, fastened on which is a plain, hand-lettered cardboard sign saying DR. LEITNER, GENERAL PRACTITIONER, DAILY 17:00–19:00 (NO ARYAN PATIENTS). The corners of Dr. Leitner's mouth turn down slightly, he knows, and in the meantime I know it too, that even Jewish patients come infrequently, more and more infrequently, that there are hardly any of them left in the city, and that he would not survive without the soups that Aunt Lisbeth takes to him daily, bravely carrying them up two flights, no matter whom she might meet on the way. That he would be lost without the piece of bread from her, without the homemade cake from Lisbeth, who loves him.

When I awake, the night must be nearly over. Kora is there again. I tell her that I didn't find the murdered infant, that maybe he really isn't lying in our cellar, she doesn't answer, she and Sister Christine are reading my temperature from the thermometer. Elvira, who, as usual, is trying to come in, is sent packing. "Not today!" She has to be washed, it's clear she's exhausted, the two of us will do it today, good thing you have the early shift again, Sister Thea. Yesterday I had the late shift, says Sister Thea, and when you change shifts, there's not much time to sleep. Her temperature is too high for this early in the morning, probably doesn't make much sense to start the cold compresses again. "What do you think, Sister Thea? Why would a twelve-year-old boy murder his brother, an infant?" "Envy and jealousy rule the world," says Sister Thea, and goes on to say that there's no one you have to be more afraid of than the disadvantaged, and if in addition they have no faith, then God help us. Sister Thea has faith, she sings in the church choir, she's – at least I think so – quite young for such unshakeable faith, but if people were at her mercy she probably wouldn't ask them about their faith or divide them up accordingly. She hears herself ask, "Sister Thea, what's going to happen to me?" and Sister Thea tells her she's sure she's going to get better. She doesn't ask the Chefarzt, who's come to tell her that the reports on the bacteria causing her fever have come in and now they can be treated with an antibiotic to which they're sensitive. "We're going to turn our big guns on them," says the Chefarzt. Dr. Knabe is already standing behind him with the syringe.

For the first time, the Chefarzt feels the need to thank her for her "excellent cooperation." That helps them a lot.

Well, where are we here, is this some kind of a business firm? And what else could she do, anyway? she asks Sister Christine later, who's of the opinion that even she might react entirely differently. She thinks that over, but can't imagine how. There appear to be unguarded moments when constant stress turns into overwhelming stress, at times something inside of her seems to be straining harder than should be necessary, but whatever the case, her heart suddenly begins to race again. She doesn't want to believe it at first, but then she has to ring anyway, unfortunately Evelyn is on duty, so it's already afternoon again, she can't find a doctor because they're all still operating, all she can do is wonder what's making her heart race, she'll try again later, but after twenty minutes the doctors from that service are still in the operating room and she's not allowed to call a doctor from another service without permission of the resident and he's just been called to O.R. 111 for an emergency, that's all Sister Evelyn knows and even after another forty minutes she doesn't know anything more, she takes the patient's pulse, astonished that she's soaking wet again, but it wouldn't make any sense to change her now, and there aren't any clean gowns anyway. Then suddenly the patient gets angry and demands that she take the initiative and find an internist immediately, doesn't matter where. Evelyn presses herself against the door indecisively until the order is repeated even more forcefully and she finally leaves. Within five minutes a young female internist comes from Ward VI with an injection. "We should have been doing this much earlier," she says, an EKG is wheeled in, the electrodes are applied, the doctor quickly locates a vein, carefully introduces the needle, and injects very slowly, while watching the oscilloscope screen, and sees, even before the patient is aware of it, her pulse rate revert to normal. "Okay," she says. "But we'll have to keep an eye on that from now on."

As a result, I'm now hooked up to yet another apparatus that displays my heartbeat as a yellow zigzag line on a monitor and beeps at the same time, more and more wires lead from my body to the outside world. When you arrive, you don't show much enthusiasm. Hello, I say, what's going on? Well, what do you think? you say and seem to have lost your sense of humor, you only want to answer questions with counter-questions, when I ask what the Chefarzt said, your taciturn reply is, What do you think? What's he supposed to say? You're starting the cold compresses again. It really has to be the work of the devil, you say. I think that's a good idea. It's just possible that it's simply the work of the devil. I'll have to think about it. But which devil? Listen, I say: Is there a devil that always wills good and always does evil?

This time you don't answer at all, just give me a look out of the corner of your eye, but you people are all wrong, not everything I say comes from febrile delusions. The devil I have in mind has arisen from the most logical of all reasoning or escaped from it during an unobserved moment in history – the dream of reason produces monsters, didn't I once hold that up to Urban, who was well enough educated to correct me: Goya called his *capricho* "The Sleep of Reason," but if I wanted to stick with dreams, it depended on who was doing the dreaming. "Yes, admittedly, when petty demons appropriate the dreams ... what then, Urban?" I asked him. "What then? Then reason is in big trouble," he said. He still owes me an answer, but I'm sure the same expression of doubt and horror was on both our faces. We'd read reports about the Rajk trial. Did the way to paradise lead unavoidably through hell?

You accomplish a slight lowering of my temperature, but today you don't want to leave. After what seems like a long time to me, I send you away, you resist, but I could easily sleep here, you say, I won't disturb you. Leave, dear, please leave.

Everything repeats itself. I can see that I'm losing the big picture. The Chefarzt thinks – now it's evening, the movable light above my bed is turned on and he's in white, so he hasn't just come from the operating room – it's not a bad sign at all if the fever can be influenced somewhat by cold compresses. From behind the carefully tended beard around his lips, cheek, and chin, Dr. Knabe says that it probably can't be considered a reaction to the operation. "Not solely," says the Chefarzt tersely. Dr. Knabe leaves, he's probably easily offended, the Chefarzt remains standing next to the bed, feels my pulse, busying himself. What am I reading there? he wants to know. I hand him the small blue book. "Goethe's poems," he says. "Hard to digest." He opens the book at the bookmark, mumbles to himself: "Never fail to exercise the power of goodness. Here crowns wend their way in eternal silence. Let them reward the industrious with abundance. We bid you hope." Then the Chefarzt says "Aha," and, after a while, "Aha" again. "With abundance," he says. "That's not badly said. Well, let's be patient until tomorrow, okay?"

Somehow comforted, he goes out. "You're fighting along with us," he says from the doorway, not waiting for an answer. Is he really on duty again, or why is he here so late in the evening? That certain pillars of support don't seem to be collapsing fills her with a restrained satisfaction, she'd like to say something like that to Kora when she finally comes in, she whispers to her she's had to think about the word "fight." Oh, says Kora. She'd do better to sleep. But she should, too! Then Kora has to laugh. "He who wants to live must fight," hopefully you don't know that one. Kora shakes her head. "And he who does not have the will to fight in this world of eternal conflict does not deserve life." A saying that hung on the wall in our school. "Yep," says Kora. "Those were some days."

Lisbeth, my Aunt Lisbeth, loved a Jewish physician in the midst of those days and had a child by him.

My God. Did you know that?

I was a child. She insisted that the father of her child sit at her side in the midst of our family during the christening. And then each one was supposed to pick a song and the Jewish doctor and illegitimate father of the baptized infant chose "By the Well Near the Gate" and my family sang it for him.

Kora remains silent.

Dr. Leitner told me himself. He came from America especially for the occasion.

Unbelievable, says Kora. Then come the tears. I begin to cry, I should have done that long ago, I cry and cry and can't stop, I cry for Lisbeth, who changed so much after the father of her child had left the country following Kristallnacht, I cry for the child, Cousin Manfred, I cry for Dr. Leitner and for our family, and I cry for myself. Kora dries my tears with a tissue. "Everything will be all right," she whispers. I shake my head. No. Nothing's going to be all right. When that's clear to me, I'm able to stop crying. "You'll make it," whispers Kora. I nod. Yes, I'll make it. I sleep.

"You're fighting along with us," says a voice that I don't recognize immediately, it takes me a while to locate it in an earlier layer of my internal archaeology, the most totally unrelated individual fragments are all too closely packed together in my head. Up, up, to the battle, to the battle / we're to the battle born. Indeed. It's Urban, Urban over and over again, who, since he's chosen to disappear in reality, has found asylum in my head. How am I to interpret his disappearance? That he's given up fighting? Unbelievable. "Him?

Never!" Renate said. "He never gives up. He'd rather beat his head against a stone wall." It was just a side issue. At the company where Urban was doing an internship as cultural secretary, the dining facilities were to be separated: one, the better one, for the executives and top employees, the other for the ordinary workers. An order from above, a measure against too much egalitarianism. Urban protested, opposed it. We watched him with apprehension, where was this going to lead. He never went to the cafeteria for the upper cadres. He was hauled up in front of the party meeting. He gave an impassioned speech. He wouldn't see it their way. "Where are we living, anyway?" he screamed. He was censured, against our three votes. But he criticized us. We should have maintained party discipline. For him it was something different, he said, for him it was a fundamental question. He was beginning to seem a little odd to me.

I have to look for him, nothing can be more urgent than going to look for him. For that I'd have to get up and I'm going to try to right now, even if they want to prevent me. First of all I have to get my left arm free, they've tied it down somewhere, I pull and twist it, there's a sticking pain in the bend of my left elbow, there's blood on my gown and the nurses won't like that. Here they come already, it would have to be Evelyn with her black curls. For God's sake, what are you doing? And here comes the next one already, Sister Christine, and trailing her, the head surgeon and Dr. Knabe. What's going on? I tell them I have to look for him. For whom? asks the Chefarzt. I say, Urban. Aha, says the Chefarzt and with an impenetrable expression, Dr. Knabe hands him my chart with the newest findings, I see how he taps several spots with his little finger, here, and here, and then there's that, too. Yes, yes, says the Chefarzt, I see, and somehow I have the feeling that he's upset with Dr. Knabe for those reports and Dr. Knabe seems to have that feeling, too. The Chefarzt says, You'll have to put off your search for a little while. I see his point. Now he wants to look at her incisions, unfortunately Sister Evelyn's on duty, the only plastic gloves available seem to be the kind that don't fit the Chefarzt or tear as soon as he puts them on. To try to lighten the atmosphere a little, the patient says "The plastic-glove aria," but she really doesn't get an amused response. Nothing wrong with the incisions, the problem can't be there. Her skin has always healed well, the patient says, and is rewarded by a hard-to-decipher look from the Chefarzt. While Evelyn is clumsily applying the wrong adhesive tape, he says, almost to himself, "I'd really love to know what's weakened your immune system this way."

That's the most important statement I've heard in a long while.

"I have to think," the Chefarzt goes on, "that the antibiotics, which are the right ones and which we're giving in sufficient dosage, are attacking those damned germs, that's obvious, that's for sure. But even they can't do everything. They're dependent on the body's own immune mechanisms."

"Yes," I say, "I can certainly see that."

The Chefarzt looks at me sympathetically and then decides to go on talking. In a dry, slightly accusatory tone, he says the course of the illness is not sufficient to explain the collapse of my immune defenses.

Aha. He's finally gotten up the gumption to give it to me straight. A word like "collapse" hasn't come up before. Every single cell in my body understands what that means.

"Maybe," I say, trying to overcome my embarrassment, "maybe the causes aren't just physical – if I had to, I could come up with a couple of other explanations – exhaustion, psychological exhaustion, I think . . ."

The Chefarzt doesn't allow himself to be affected by my stammering. He becomes completely official now, entirely impersonal. Another look with the CAT scanner – just a brief one – turns out to be necessary. They can still do it today. Quite brief, as mentioned. He doesn't look at me, he's speaking to Dr. Knabe, who's already aware of all that, even I look away tactfully, it appears that this time my consent is not being sought for what's going to happen, then does happen in an atmosphere of greatly embarrassed detachment, without anyone's taking notice of me. Sister Christine puts on her bland head-nurse expression, changes the I.V. bottles, puts in a new infusion catheter, everything quickly, deftly, says that today we're going to have intermittent thunderstorms again, and with a single gesture gets rid of Elvira, who insists on emptying the trash bucket. The young male nurse, Jürgen, who is mopping up the floor with a disinfectant solution, appears to have become a bit too chipper out of embarrassment and is complaining that this year he hasn't even been able to sit out in front of his father's boathouse until just recently. And even Sister Thea, who appears on duty punctually in the afternoon, who always sees at a glance what has to be done, pulls the blind because the sun is directly in front of the window, pushes the roll under my knees, and changes my gown – even Sister Thea doesn't let herself get involved in conversation.

I have trouble with the word "collapse." I see images of hell, but for what sin? I have no use for religion, which tries to convince us that the cause of every misfortune is guilt, but why misfortune, am I involved in a misfortune? Kora says she wouldn't exactly call it a piece of good fortune, but she'd prefer if I didn't go on talking now, maybe if I didn't think so much I'd be able to sleep, I'll buy that, but unfortunately, while she's still standing at my bedside, I feel a slight shaking starting up inside me, not again, I won't have it, I try to resist, tense my muscles, clench my teeth, but it's stronger than I am, it breaks my resistance, seizes me, shakes me, shakes the bed, makes my teeth chatter. Punitive action, I think. Wailing and gnashing of teeth. So that's what that means. Kora has already pressed the call bell, Sister Thea is already throwing a second blanket over me, pushing my shaking shoulders down, how banal these repetitions are, how comfortless, the oxygen tank is already in the room, Kora slips the mask over my nose and mouth: breathe, breathe, deep breath!

THIS IS THE POINT OF NO RETURN. Huge, flaming letters on a dark wall.

No. Not that, too. Not the harsh clanking of weapons, too. If I'd only been more gratefully aware of the preceding quiet. Next time, I'll be grateful for the silence and the absence of images in my head. Now I have to endure the infernal noise and the columns of the tormented who drag themselves through history and look out at me from within me. Not accusingly. Suffering. I'm standing face to face with the sufferers. I only manage to do that at times when I'm suffering myself. The secret meaning of suffering occurs to me. I know I'll forget it again.

Why has your immune system collapsed? Perhaps, Herr Professor, because it has stepped in and taken charge of the collapse that the person could not allow herself to be responsible for. Because it slyly – that's just the way those forces within us happen to be – laid the person low, made her sick, in order to pull her away from death's undertow in this somewhat roundabout and laborious way and push the responsibility off on someone else, namely you, Herr Professor. Was that the reason for your embarrassment just now, for your scarcely concealed displeasure? That you reject the role that threatens to fall to you now? Because you're beginning to get an inkling about this person's intentions, concealed from her, herself, which, incidentally, can't really be called intentions? The way she, too, would rather not talk or think about a collapse, but about being relieved, about the strong urge to disappear, which that mysterious immune system is carrying out as her stand-in, and which, in turn, like so many things we believe in, is also just a projection, an abstraction, banished into words, so that we can have peace and quiet, go on living, untroubled, without paying attention to the traces that our unscrupulousness and ignorance have left behind in our bodies. In the immune system, for example, that might some day see itself forced to desert us. That might be fed up with its role as supervisor, watchman, and pursuer, simply fed up with always being on the trail of some more or less evil-intentioned agent and, as a result, even having to put up with being maligned by the expression "killer cells." That saw through the manipulations of this crafty person and simply lay down and went to sleep when the infection was just beginning, microscopically small and – if someone had only paid attention to it – easily controllable. And that simply couldn't see any reason to behave any more intelligently, alertly, reasonably, or more desirous of living than the person herself. "Self," what a tottering, blurred concept.

Her body had given notice promptly enough, but at the first attack of searing pain she didn't want to believe anything bad was going on, didn't want to call the doctor or interrupt her trip, and offered her "overstressed" stomach chamomile tea, but how is it to be explained that, weeks later, when the pains were even more severe, the nausea even worse, and just getting a sip of tea down was absolutely out of the question, she still didn't want a doctor, was still

Not inappropriate is the matter-of-fact way that Sister Christine goes about her business, wearing her nurse's smile over an inscrutable face, her routine is being carried out, well-practiced procedures, she knows her job, I go along with the game. Have I gone along too often in similar situations, is my body trying to tell me that? Kora, the dark woman, isn't hiding from the situation. She's waiting for me in the prep room next to the O.R., failing to conceal a certain amount of anxiety, but even she doesn't have much to say, only that I can depend on the team. The team's depending on me. Depending on, the double meaning of the words. I don't say much, either. I say okay. Sister Nadeshda is following Kora's directions carefully, she seems to have lost her ability to speak German but not her Russian smile.

"Cut," "Cut into," "Make a cut": I seem to have some affinity for the double meanings of words. "Oh, you've cut yourself." As a matter of fact, Urban has been cutting me for quite some time, being seen with me would have caused him problems. When was that, anyway? It was during all that business with Paul, I haven't thought about that for such a long time.

Paul, a little guy, a bit too zealous but absolutely loyal and dependable, Paul, whom we all liked and at the same time didn't take completely seriously and whom Urban, when he was given a higher post at the ministry, summoned to his side as a sort of personal advisor and jack of all trades, to everyone's amazement. And who turned out to be the very one entrusted with the execution of a plan that he, Urban, had cooked up, the last part of which was to be an official announcement that several of us were to have collaborated on and which was intended to introduce a radically new youth policy. We should have known that nothing good was going to come of it, but Urban may well have known and used Paul as the fall guy. When he ended up being punished and disappeared "to Orcus," as word from those around Urban would have it, Urban was a bit shaken, too, but whom would it have helped if he'd been toppled as well? For a while, at any rate, he had to distance himself from people who weren't as pure as the driven snow. Renate called sometimes to plead for understanding for him. The easy relationship between us was gone for good. Paul, however, who became ill and disappeared into a sanatorium for months, Paul, who remained dependable and true to himself, never recovered. He's doing menial work in some archive.

The Professor comes as usual, he's not cowardly, just stingy with his words. And suffering from this damned, contagious embarrassment. He shakes hands, politely as usual. Yes, I've had the injection, the slight, pleasant buzzing in my head is starting. "Can we?" I say, "We can." "Good," he says. He disappears, green on green, behind the door of the operating room. Minutes later, when I follow – actually I'm being followed, but you can't talk that way – the three men in green are standing there, silent and motionless, their hands raised in surrender, their eyes fixed on me. Who's attacking whom here? Who's surrendering to whom? I have surrendered myself / my heart and hands / to you, O life and love-filled land / my one and only fatherland. A black-framed saying, above my grandparents' sofa.

As always, Kora's brown eyes above her face mask are the last thing I see. Mask. Then the system of corridors, the nervous system? Familiar, but not on intimate terms. Couldn't ever become intimate, but more familiar each time. Down, into the depths, past the pale green metal box. BIG BROTHER. "You have to live with it," Urban once said to me. "We have to live with it everywhere in the world." At some point he'd begun to say "we" in that new, almost con-

spiratorial way. "We," he said secretively, suspected by his
own people in his own country, belonging to a larger broth-
erhood that provided him with comfort and justification
and exerted a strong, seductive force. Upon me, too? Yes.
Upon me, too. For some time they'd been living in their real
city with that metal box in the cellar into which their telephone line disappeared suspiciously, and, simultaneously,
in another city of hope and humanity that was their actual
home, or would be, that we were already seizing from the
future, that we would create for ourselves, the "we" that even
Urban meant. When had she stopped feeling that she was
being addressed when he said "we"? I don't believe there
was any single, particular incident, just an accumulation of
everyday and less-everyday incidents that caused the per-
sistent pain and forcibly led to those insights that Urban
shrank from. And it was not one of the most trivial pains
when she realized that he'd set himself up for the long haul
in some three room apartment on Karl Marx Allee with
Renate and in an office in some ministry or other. From
which he'd now escaped, fled, this time forever – about that
she'd never had a second's doubt. And with that flight, had
taken refuge again in the realm of her understanding.
Incurable situation.

Expose, be exposed. Exposing the entrails, from which
the modern augurs are unable to read anything, neither sal-
vation nor the opposite. My revulsion toward the exposure
of others, against self-exposure. The intimacy of the situation, which is made "objective" through a cleverly devised
ritual. The cuts. Made according to a prescribed pattern,
anything else would be an artistic blunder. "He who will not
hear must feel," Grandmother's words. He who can't feel
must be hurt more severely. And whoever can't bring himself to cut, or can't cut deeply enough, into his own flesh

provides the excuse for someone else to do it for him, Herr Professor. The staging and preparations, all full of tricks. How often the "soul," the "consciousness," whatever they might be, lay there helplessly, exposed to manipulation. Now the body's being manipulated, to finally give the word its due. Worked on by hand. By skilled, schooled, and trained hands, washed for fifteen minutes and shielded by plastic gloves. That attempt to get to the bottom of the truth of the body, which has been hidden for so long. That rummaging around in the intestines. Proceeding according to a well thought-out strategy, taking a cunning detour in order to press on, without injuring other organs, to the root of the trouble, to the locus of the abscess, the place where the glowing nucleus of the truth coincides with the glowing nucleus of the lie. Is identical to, whether you want to admit that or not, Professor. While Sister Nadeshda retracts the edges of the incision or goes into action with a sponge. While Kora watches over her apparatus, now and again stroking my forehead. A massacre.

"I believe we've gotten it all this time." Where am I? The awakener's classic question, to which one can only be given a trite answer or none at all. Sister Thea simply gives my room number, as in a hotel. The Professor, entirely in green, has to leave, announces however that he'll be back soon. "I'm sure we've gotten it all this time."

You come in. What time is it? Oh, afternoon already? Waking up, I say to you with a paralyzed tongue, is always miraculous. Everything's over and you haven't noticed a thing. It'd be even better if . . . you say. Dr. Knabe comes in and asks Sister Thea about my temperature. "Well, okay," he says. It'd be even better if . . . "This time," he says, "we got it all. There's nothing left. There can't be anything left." He turns the door handle over to the senior surgeon who's come to tell me that this time there can't be anything left. "As far as it's humanly possible to tell," he says. I ask you why you aren't laughing. You say, Later. I say, Good. But sometime or other we have to laugh again.

By the way, I say, I think the labyrinth in my brain corresponds with the labyrinth in our cellar system. You get a shocked look. No, I say, I'm not imagining that. It's just that I'm always wandering around in those subterranean passageways, can't you see that? You say, does it have to be that way? I say, I believe it does. Anyway, tell me, have they found Urban yet? You get your blank expression and shake your head. I can see that you don't want to tell me and I don't want to know. I say, Once he told me that truth was relative, do you remember? You shake your head. The truth, Urban had said, that's years ago, was a function of progress in history. Anything else was just emotional kitsch. Was he trying to say that the end justified the means? He hesitated. Then he said, To a certain degree. To what degree? she'd then asked, and he, still whispering, since they were surrounded by other people in the commuter train: That had to be decided case by case. She: And who did the deciding? And Urban: Always has to be the ones who can see the big picture best. At any rate, according to their expertise and not the criteria of their moral rigor. That would disarm us, couldn't she see that? In that case we might as well hang out the white flag right away. Or? She said, whispering, I don't know. I really don't know. And he: Think it over.

Sometime or other, you left. Sister Thea doesn't seem to have much to do, every couple of minutes she comes into the room, checks the I.V., rearranges the head end of the bed so it's more comfortable, wipes her face with a cold compress, swabs her lips and mouth. "Tomorrow," she says, "everything will seem entirely different. But of course, you know that, you're a pro." When the Professor comes, all in white, she's just taken her temperature, she holds the thermometer out toward him. "Well, there we are," he says. "That already looks a bit more promising. Of course we'll go on with the injections, Sister Thea, every five hours if you'd be so kind. It would be even worse if we didn't finish those fellows off." Even Sister Thea is convinced that we're finishing those fellows off now. I hardly notice it when she gives me the injection. Too bad she doesn't have the night shift, but she'll be there first thing in the morning again.

Happily enough, Kora has the night duty, Kora Bachmann, she comes when it's dark. This time she says, "The masters of the art have really done their work. There's nothing left, I'll stick my hand in the fire if I'm wrong." I look at Kora's hand, it's narrow and very feminine, for the first time it occurs to me that she could have children. I ask her, she nods. A girl, four years old, Luise. And who takes care of her when she's working? My mother, whenever Luise's not at kindergarten. And the father? Divorced, says Kora. I say, That's a shame. After a while, she says she sometimes thinks men and women go together less and less in our part of the world. Then we both fall silent. Kora has to go. She'll come back. "Sleep," she says.

I've already lost enough time sleeping, taking everything into account I'm losing a lot of time in here. Much later I'll understand that that's my first communication from the cosmos of the healthy. When becoming healthy means not looking upon being sick as the only possible condition. I restrain myself. I'm not that far. On the well-known rails of dreams I glide, almost relieved, into that parallel realm where I feel quite well, why, I can't ask, but something within me knows the answer: because all thoughts are suspended, all differentiation ceases, good and bad, true and false, right and wrong no longer count. Recovery for the overstressed conscience. The color is gray. The dark woman has taken me by the hand, no one can make out who's leading whom, she smiles and says something like "For the last time," I'm already feeling regret, even though that last time still lies ahead of me. The window of our Berlin room again, out of which we float, that's the way it has to be. The courtyard below us, imprisoned within the walled quadrangle of buildings. Above us, the rectangle of sky that, here in the middle of the city, never becomes completely dark. The sharply demarcated traces of light in a few windows. The garish music from the top floor. Everything as usual and everything new. We let ourselves down, float through the entry portal, both sides of which, curiously, are standing wide open.

Friedrichstrasse is torn up. Deep ditches run along the edges of the sidewalks, bordered by big piles of sand and rocks. Still floating, we follow the course of the ditches and look into the tangle of cables and pipes below us. Exposed entrails. Yes, says Kora, you could call it that. We glide by late-night visitors who come out of the Little Revue, slightly tipsy, and at the corner of Hannover and Chausseestrasse we sit down on one of the sand piles that the machines have thrown up. A spectral light shines up out of the underworld. On the nearly vertical sides of the ditches we can read off the layers in which the decades have piled their debris. The archaeology of destruction. Kora, who's still holding my hand, gives me a signal, we lower ourselves into the ditch, down to the lowest level that the excavator has exposed. Into Hades, I say to Kora. The god of the underworld who abducted beautiful Persephone on his golden chariot. But grief and refusal to work on the part of her inconsolable mother, Demeter, had the result that she, the daughter, was permitted to be with her for two-thirds of the year, in the bright upper world, whose fertility depended on her.

Kora never learned Greek mythology at school. We're standing on cracked, smashed flagstones, a wall tile displays green vines, another, sausages linked together. An old-style butcher shop from the previous century, we presume, buried under. By means of gentle scraping, we expose a higher layer – bricks, in which Cyrillic letters are scratched, I decipher a name, Pavel was here, I tell Kora. She can read Russian, too. Vladimir came from Novgorod, she says. Maybe he would have preferred to stay there. Messages from a submerged epoch. How fast it goes, I whisper to Kora. And the later ones are always quick to cover the traces of the past with their cobblestones and concrete, on which the new soldiers then march. And if we were to dig a little and work our way into the walls, we'd come across bones. The pock marks in the walls above and below ground are evidence of a heavy exchange of gunfire, obviously human flesh must have gotten in the way of the bullets.

We don't dig. We move further along the system of ditches, following water and drainage lines, some of which gurgle, some of which come to a dead end, rusted shut, we come across cable conduits in which the wires have long since rotted and beside which – that's the reason for these excavations – new wires are being laid in new conduits, through which power will flow, through which telephone conversations will go back and forth, some being listened in on, some not, and someday, after another half-century, to which I'll no longer be a witness, these ditches will have to be opened again and others, who haven't yet been born, will stand here and wrack their brains trying to figure out what their ancestors could have had in mind.

Forget about that, says Kora, who can read minds it would seem, I'm not really surprised. Don't brood. But, I say, when you think about how everything always repeats itself. Now you're becoming trite, says Kora, she uses such words, it would seem. And anyway, she adds, for those experiencing it for the first time, every repetition is new. Aha. I hold my tongue politely. She's trying to cheer me up. She's been assigned to lead me out of the blind alley in which I'm apparently stuck. And she doesn't hesitate to use cheap tricks. I put her to the test: Does she know a word like "futility"? She snorts through her nose a little. Every doctor knows that word, and how! A miss is as good as a mile, I say, and Kora laughs. What I mean, I say – and she, who's forgotten all of her politeness and all of her renowned empathy, brusquely interrupts me. Says she knows exactly what I mean: that great, all-encompassing futility in which you can roll around so wonderfully and lull yourself to sleep so splendidly. Now it's my turn to laugh. But if it makes sense anyway? If this, considered quite soberly, is the sum total of life: futility? Now just listen, says Kora. We've risen out of the ditch and are floating down Friedrichstrasse, we veer to the left down Unter den Linden, the whole place devoid of people, there are only a few nocturnal Wartburgs wandering like poor souls in this extinct city, for which I suddenly have an exceptionally warm feeling. Now listen, this is simply not the right moment to trot out all your mistakes, says Kora. On the left-hand side, the university flies by, scarcely time to wave to the two Humboldts. The arsenal. Kora, I say, that's not something you can judge. Why not, she says, because I'm younger than you are? That, too, I say. And because you're my doctor. In other words, not without prejudice? she says. Now she's getting angry, I wouldn't have expected that of her at all. Then she might as well just go. She pulls her hand away from mine. Not yet, I say.

Suddenly we're sitting on the steps of the Palace of the

Republic. Another pile of rock, too, I think, glass and concrete, built only to perish. For that reason, perhaps, the most honest place in this perishing city tonight. Metropolis. Metropole of power. Metropole of two powers. The city, once a holy place, deconsecrated. It's falling apart in front of our eyes. And no turning back out of the new wilderness. The certainty tears at my heart.

Kora, I say, someone's put you up to this, haven't they? Kora tells me I really have a nasty mind. Now she's sad. Yes, I say, I have an evil mind and now you know what I meant by futility. If you ride the tiger, you never get off. And now go and tell your Chief something about my broken-down immune system. Ask him if he knows those old maps with all the white areas where people simply wrote "*hic sunt leones.*" Ask him if, when he was cutting into my flesh, when he was opening my incisions and exposing my rotten places, he came upon any of those white spots, unknown even to me, that are unexplored and unnamed, ruled by wild animals. Ask him whether he's capable of imagining that every immune mechanism in the world will come to grief against those resistant spots.

Whom shall I ask what? Oh, Kora, where are we? Where we always are, my dear, and your gown is drenched with sweat again. The night nurse comes in and without much fuss they've changed her, both of them claim that this perspiration has a very different smell. Healthier, they think. Didn't you notice that yourself? asks Kora. Still acting on someone's behalf? What are you talking about? Shouldn't dwell on things? No. You shouldn't. You should rejoice about everything that's finally behind you and you should decide to get well. Decide? Yes, indeed, says Kora emphatically. Decide firmly and never deviate from the decision. Well, okay. Her oath right into God's ear. They laugh. Kora leaves.

Elvira awakens her. She takes her position, surveys the room, then the patient, satisfied, it seems to the latter. She makes the racket with the trash bucket, walks over to her bed, shakes her hand. "Well," she says in conclusion. "That was close. You could easily have kicked off, right?"

What should I say to that, or think? That you only really know what you get to hear? He who will not hear must feel, but I can't manage to feel. That sentence of Elvira's has a considerable aftereffect. To give way to panic now would be ridiculous. Elvira really only said what I myself must have known. I can only be amazed at the number of disguises truth uses to hide itself from weak people and in what curious shapes it appears when the time is right. They did all let me know some time ago, the physicians with their impenetrable expressions, the nurses with their bustling around, and not last of all, even you, my dear, with your reticence. But I wasn't able to take in the message, something within me warned the truth against appearing unveiled. Then Elvira comes in and spills what she's overheard in the nurses' lounge and in the kitchen and out comes this crude, naked sentence. It's true. Unfortunately. Even panic arrives late, like everything else.

But why, really? The calamity has been fended off, the aura of misfortune can disappear. Instead of that, it increases, grows and grows, until it has completely filled me. The collapse after the danger has been surmounted, a hackneyed old story. And now I'm sitting on that old horse that's carried me across Lake Constance. I must have said something of the sort to the Professor, who just looked in briefly, already in green, to hear Sister Margot's reassuring report about my condition. "Lake Constance?" he asks irritatedly and looks over at Sister Margot who shrugs her shoulders slightly and draws the corners of her mouth down. "I get it.

Lake Constance. But what's brought that up?" "Isn't it true?" "True, true," says the Professor brusquely. "Every person has his or her own truth, you should know that." "And you know mine?" "But of course. It goes like this: You were sick, very sick, and now you've come through it. You've made it. It's all clear sailing from here. And anything else is rubbish."

I won't get my Professor to say words like "death" and "die," which are flitting through my head while Sister Margot and Sister Thea are washing me, making my bed, and at the same time talking incessantly to me about happy subjects, even about Sister Margot's unsuccessful attempts to lose weight, quite fitting, I say, at the bedside of someone who's been on a hunger strike, they laugh, today they're taking everything lightly, have been told to, that's clear to me, and they know that I know. I can just see the Professor standing in the hallway with them, saying to Margot, "Just be careful that she doesn't crash on us now, if you'd be so kind." I call after Sister Thea, "Hey, in the hospital maybe you don't talk about death." She spins around, looks me straight in the eye and says "No."

Now you know, says someone triumphantly within me. But I don't want to know. Do I even want to make the effort of coming back, of distancing myself laboriously, step by step, from that portal in front of which I was deposited, without moving a muscle, by a tide that I can hardly remember? I still remember – soon I'll forget them – the moments during which the least bit of agreement, the slightest yielding would have sufficed to wash me through that gateway forever. To be gone for good, without regret. I've missed that moment. But why did I withhold my consent? Now I'm tired. Soon I'll give myself over to sleep again. Didn't I once make a resolution to be grateful if I'd been spared from the din long enough? I try to be grateful, but I don't know how.

It will come back eventually, says a comforting voice, invading my sleep. It will all come back. The sailboat, in which I'm bobbing across a beautiful lake, bears the name *Esperanza*.

Well, I think as I awaken, slightly amused, it didn't have to be quite so blatantly obvious. You're standing there and don't want to talk about anything but my noontime temperature, which is only slightly elevated, and about how satisfied the Professor is with my condition. You don't even want to hear what Elvira said to me this morning. I'm simply not to take such backward-looking oracles seriously. You put a bouquet where I can see it, each individual blossom is from our garden, you remind me where each of them came from, you list off the flowers that will still be blooming when I come home, soon. Vaguely, the image of returning home rises up before my eyes, but I let it fade out immediately, because for me to ever take a step outside of this bed is unimaginable. I say, You were probably really worried about me. You stand at the window, looking out at the landscape – which I haven't seen yet – and say, What kind of a thought is that? Anyway, it hasn't rained for three whole days. Maybe they'll be able to save something of the harvest.

What kind of a thought is that? What occurs to me is that I'm not actually thinking about anything. Actually I haven't thought about anything for the longest time, without missing thinking. Actually, I've felt quite well without thinking. I say that to you, you turn around and wrinkle your forehead. Well okay, felt well, I say. Everything's relative. Yeah, you say, and nothing more, but in that tone of voice that still provokes me, after all these years. All I mean, I say, is that thinking can be so painful that you exchange it on the sly for other pains. A kind of horse-trading with yourself, as it were. Silence. So that's the kind of theory you're fiddling around with now. It just occurred to me. You don't think it's so good, I take it? The word "good" doesn't suit you. I have the impression you'd like to banish it from my surroundings for a while, it doesn't seem to have stood the test of time. It's okay with me. Let's talk about the lesser evil. In other words, my thinking is the greater evil for me? I'll have to think that one over, I say, and attempt a sort of grin. I know what you're thinking: Nothing can be a greater evil than death, but you don't say it. We remain silent a while, during which each of us knows what the other is thinking, and we arrive at the same point simultaneously. Listen, I say, have they found Urban?

I can tell by looking at you that you've been expecting the question and that it goes against the grain. Why am I always going on about Urban? Yes. They found him. Dead. I knew that. I don't ask how he died. Not today. Actually, it wasn't really so bad when I was still so weak, I could send every visitor, even you, away after a little while. Have you spoken with Renate? I ask. You say no. No reason given. If I'd been at home, I'd have had to talk to her. Over the course of the years those divisions of labor make themselves obvious. After a while I say, We've really gotten pretty old, don't you think? You say, We'll make it a little while longer. I say, without real conviction, If you think so.

Something's bothering me. When you're gone, I realize what: I'm again starting to tell you what you want to hear. The time of not having to be considerate is past. I know what that means, but don't want to admit it yet. Anyway, the last time we saw Renate was at Jutta's wedding. All of us considered it obvious that she'd come to say goodbye to Jutta and that Urban was not coming. Denmark, she said, none of us had ever been to Denmark, the young Danish diplomat with whom Jutta was going away was appealing, and actually he didn't quite know what he'd gotten himself into, but he'd been taught to help if he could. And if this pretty young woman could only leave her country if he married her, then that's what he was going to do and he treated her friends – who didn't all look as happy as they should at a wedding – to Danish goodies and watched while they all danced with his young wife, whom he wouldn't touch, of course not, and she'd be able to translate for him everywhere and wouldn't be a burden to him, of course not. Later, around midnight, Urban showed up anyway. He wanted to pick up Renate – she really did have to be at work early the next morning. Renate shook her head. We attempted to be completely at ease with Urban, which resulted in his going over to the improvised bar where he proceeded to get drunk. That was the only time you ever got involved with him. You walked over to him and said Beat it! Urban turned on his heels and left. Much later we took Renate home in a taxi, none of us said a word.

"You don't need to take it," I tell Sister Thea. "I don't have a fever." "Good girl," she says. "You couldn't have said anything nicer to me. This is really a time for rejoicing, isn't it?" I really have to say that Sister Thea is a dear person, I'm sure she prayed for me, and tonight she'll thank her God. She's full of optimistic prophecies. "Soon be rid of that," she points at the new I.V. bottle as she hangs it. "Yes, and this whole plumbing system as well," she announces while she's checking to see what's come out of my various drains. She considers the whole business repulsive. I'm hearing that from her for the first time, until this point she's always been professional – even kindly – in the way she's expressed herself about all the tubes that go into me one place and come out another. "But you can't take my intravenous away," I say, almost fearfully, "I'll starve." Then Sister Thea becomes sarcastic, something I would never have expected of her. "Normal people eat with their mouths," she says. "Forgotten already?"

What's wrong with her? Afraid of starving? The Professor has to laugh indulgently, Sister Thea told him about it. The patient's temperature doesn't interest him at all, she's almost offended. "Starve!" he says. "Not a pretty way to die, either. Let's just stay away from that, all right? Just let us take care of everything."

"Not much else I can do."

"That's right," he says. "At the moment, not much else you can do. But up to this point things have gone pretty well for you, haven't they?"

He wants to hear a little praise for his good work, there hasn't been any of that so far. Something must have changed in this hospital room, everyone's showing her a different face today. Aware of her obligation, she says, "Yes, you've really taken good care of me." Now he's embarrassed, her Professor, and quickly says goodbye. But before he goes, in the doorway, he adds, "I'm a lot more pleased with you this evening."

Urban's dead and they're a lot more pleased with me. Soon they'll be so pleased with me that I won't get any of their searching looks anymore, they won't admonish me to be patient and cooperate. They won't pay such close attention anymore because they're no longer expecting any nasty surprises from me. From Urban we weren't expecting any nasty surprises, either, or any happy ones. On the contrary, I'd written him off. That has to be said plainly. Urban had become someone who went along with everything and would go along with everything in the future, too. Until – to everyone's surprise – something finally came up that even he couldn't go along with. There's actually a gleam of hope in that, but maybe not. The problem is that sometimes even hope runs out, has to run out, that has to be admitted, too. When did he realize that? Suddenly, when they demanded that he retract the speech he'd given the previous day, a fairly radical speech, the product of his despair, as Renate had said on the phone? Despair about what? That everything will be lost if we don't turn back now. Late, I said, late, too late. Or did I only think that, in order not to hurt her even more. In any case, the answer came from her, very softly: Despair over the fact that he didn't offer any opposition earlier. And I again, softly: And why didn't he? Because he thought that then everything really would be lost, said Renate, and began to cry uncontrollably.

Actually he was too smart for that. In other words, he'd been in a difficult spot for an even longer time. Urban, whom I once liked very much, whom I liked less and less as the years went by. Whom I wrote off – as if I had a surplus of friends – instead of . . . instead of what? Talking with him? Even now, even after it's come to this, I know that would have been senseless. The way out that he chose, that chose him, was one I'd rejected. I fended off the temptation. Basically we differ a lot, Urban and I, I've known that for a long time. Let him know it, too. I could forgive such conduct, I told him, from people dumber than he. Not from him. After that he completely avoided having anything to do with me. And I avoided having anything to do with him. Our orbits no longer touched, not even at the bad points. That was the most comfortable arrangement, for both of us.

Because gradually the realization dawned on us that you either had to sacrifice yourself or that which they call "the cause," formerly "our common cause," the modifiers having been dropped, one by one. That realization placed a string of years in a distinct light.

Kora says what she always says: You think too much. You

talk too much. Give it a rest. Kora's privileges are revoked.

From the radio, the dark tone of a clarinet, there's still that. She falls asleep and dreams of nothing at all, awakens when the night nurse comes in with the thermometer, falls asleep again, doesn't notice that the thermometer's being taken out, sleeps through Elvira's noisy entrance and the first brief visit of the Professor, which Sister Christine tells her about. Says he was delighted and that the sun was shining outside. Perhaps the harvest can be saved after all. But now she can even wash her face herself, can't she, since her arm isn't hooked up to the I.V.? She agrees completely with Sister Christine and does what she tells her to. When she's gone, she immediately falls asleep again, wakes up, falls asleep, sees the sunbeam appear on the wall, sees it move during the intervals when she's not asleep, then disappear, then you're standing next to the bed, saying your child is sleeping her way back to health. I say I'm so tired. No wonder, you say. But I really think it is a wonder.

I talk about caverns in which feelings arise. I can't say where I know that from. I realize that I can't convey every experience to you with words. Actually they don't arise, our feelings. They thaw out. As if they'd been frozen solid. Or anesthetized.

Anesthetized by what?

By the shock that everything that I say or write is distorted by what I don't say and don't write.

That's normal, my love, you say. We'll save that for later, okay?

Yes. How did Urban die?

He hanged himself. In the woods. He wasn't found until weeks had gone by.

Renate, my God, Renate. She'll have to live with that image.

You say you've called her. She hardly spoke.

You tell me he'd been relieved of his duties in front of the entire staff. His institute would be taken over by someone else. He had another attack of his pig-headedness, went into a rage, stormed out of the meeting, and drove off in his car. He parked it somewhere or other. They found a note on the seat: You'll never find me.

Now that's enough for today. Yes, I say, and fall asleep. As I awaken, I have this sentence in my ear: All that's transitory is just a metaphor. She quotes that sentence to Kora Bachmann, who's just come in. "They were pretty clever, people back then," she says.

"By the way, we actually have the same profession. You track down pain in the body, I do it in other places."

"In the soul, you mean."

"It occurs to me that your surgeons never find the soul, no matter how deeply they cut. And therefore they don't believe in it."

The Professor wants to know what it is that he doesn't believe in, he's been standing in the doorway. "Oh, the soul," he says good-naturedly, as if he's talking about some adorable little animal. "Oh yes we do, we take it very seriously."

"What?"

It finally comes out. The soul as troublemaker. That shouldn't be underestimated. There are cases whose outcome can't be explained by anything other than non-physical disruptive forces.

"You suspected those in my case."

The Professor becomes professional. Says in her case it was unequivocally the germs. "Bacteria that we brought to their senses."

"And what's with my weak immune system?"

"Yes, well," says the Professor and shrugs his shoulders.

The two women laugh at him, he laughs along with them. "We'll get after your immune system, too." But if he might allow himself a question, does she still have any pain?

She tunes in to her painful locations, hears nothing. "Well, there you are," says the Professor, "isn't that good news?" He starts to put on the plastic gloves that Sister Margot hands him. Two pairs tear as soon as he puts his fingers into them. For the first time, she hears him curse. "It's always the same," he says, "they can't even make a decent pair of gloves anymore." She mustn't ask him whom he means by "they." Dr. Knabe, who has the night duty and who's been standing at the foot of her bed for a while, puts it more clearly. It's part of his personality to be a proclaimer of gloom. He speaks of shortages, of decline, and dissolution. Or perhaps it shouldn't be considered scandalous that nursing units such as this one don't have enough gowns to be able to give the patients fresh ones. "You can't imagine," he says, "how we have to improvise every day here. How's her temperature by the way?"

It seems to her that they've all been waiting for the moment when they can neglect her temperature and all the other symptoms of illness in order to let their own problems take center stage. She's not sure she likes that. You can get used to having all the attentiveness and concern directed at you. It occurs to her that she has a right to be tired. She makes that clear to Dr. Knabe, who leaves immediately, and she falls asleep. There's that homunculus in front of me again, it's floating unconcernedly through the subterranean corridors in its bluish light. A feeling, for which I've been searching for a name, rises up within me while I'm being forced to follow the light that's now shining on names scratched into the old cellar walls, names that mean nothing to me. Suddenly I recognize the names of dead relatives and the feeling becomes stronger. Then it's right there, next to a rickety lattice door, scrawled on the sooty wall with chalk: Hannes Urban. Now I recognize the feeling: it's horror. The light's trying to pull me through the lattice door. Then something screams Stop! and I'm hurled back by the echo.

"Having a bad dream?" asks Elvira. I can still hear the scream. Elvira says she never dreams and doesn't scream in her sleep, either. I'd almost gotten to see something then that I would never have been able to forget.

Elvira thinks Sister Thea is good. She's the best nurse of all, who's the best of the doctors she can't say, she hardly ever sees them and if she does, they don't pay any attention to her. As far as the doctors are concerned, says Elvira proudly, there's only the medical personnel and, of course, the patients. That's the way it has to be. Yes, she gets up really early to get here on time, even before the day shift nurses, luckily the streetcar goes right by her building, and getting up early doesn't bother her, her boyfriend has to get up early, too, he has a good job as a potato peeler and vegetable scrubber in the company kitchen, where he gets his meals too, good, nourishing ones. He's respected there, believe you me. The two of them have it really good, says Elvira. Here on the nursing floor everyone's nice to her, too. And just think of all the things she's learned here! "Well, so long, have a good day."

Time jumps onto its tracks. Times of day take on form, morning, noon, evening, from morning and evening a new day is made. Night stands out in sharp contrast. Even the doctors have definite times, they don't come to see her any more often than they do the other patients, only the Professor sticks with his habit of coming in early for a quick look, before the first operation. "Things going okay? How was your night?"

The little radio begins to speak, occasionally it reads

something to her out loud. That's a good thing, because she still can't hold a book. Once it says in a practiced, measured voice, "Death is really one of the main processes of life." That makes sense to her, but then again it doesn't. That's really only valid if death has drawn back, or what do you think? So that life can then step forward all the more brilliantly, right? You haven't thought about that much, you don't think life needs death as a background against which to show more brilliantly or whatever. Kora Bachmann, who's also coming less often, might construe the sentence otherwise, namely, that life uses death as a means to tear those who are tired of life, or fed up with it, out of their criminal lethargy, to push them back into life by means of therapeutic terror, so that they'll get back on course again and know why they're on earth.

But why, exactly, Kora? Well, to live. There you have it, I say.

Kora leaves. I say, She's not exactly to your liking. Why would you say that? You know why. Because she changes everything to fit her own point of view. You take offense at that. You don't accept that. Claim you'd thought what Kora said was actually right, but anyway, you don't know her well enough. As if that ever prevented you from passing judgment. You just have to contradict that, I stick to my guns, then we realize that we're starting to argue, have to laugh, and agree that I couldn't have shown any more clearly that my health is returning.

On the following day, the pathologist comes in, unannounced. She's not prepared for his visit, but of course she can't refuse to see him. Why should she, anyway? A sort of courtesy call, judging by the way he enters. Nattily dressed under the spotless white coat that he wears open. Silver tie. Slender, if not actually gaunt, extends a thin hand toward her. A cold, lifeless handshake. "Well," he says with a slightly hoarse voice, the ambassador from the underworld, and waits for her to laugh. He doesn't laugh. She's often been wheeled past the sign in the basement corridor, she says, the one with the white arrow pointing to pathology. "Past," he says. "That's good. That's very good." Now he's smiling, but she'd rather not see that smile. Hollow cheeks that have to be shaved at least twice a day but still don't lose their bluish cast, a shock of jet-black hair cut with painful precision, the tip of which falls low on his forehead. Everyone knows from television, of course, what it looks like in a pathology department these days – cold, rigid bodies under white sheets or in the cooler, the sight of which is bearable because people don't relate it to themselves, she thinks in a sort of premonitory panic. But, but, says her visitor, he doesn't have anything at all to do with that, almost nothing at any rate, and gives no word of explanation about how he knows what she's just been thinking. That's how people are, says the pathologist, they make those they've saddled with things that someone has to do pay for their own unreasonableness. Yes, it was that way, she agreed immediately, he was no doubt right, that's the way people were. He, a person who'd been given things to do that someone had to, twisted his mouth into a grimace that was at once pained and scornful. But aside from that, though she probably wouldn't believe it, he'd come out of curiosity. He wanted to see the woman who'd bred such dangerous little beasts in her body. He'd had them under the microscope, you see, had isolated and identified them, quite unique specimens that even an experienced man like him didn't get to see every day. "Enterobacteriaciae."

Now she felt the need to be humorous. Should she be proud of her accomplishment? she wanted to know. He stared at her, weighing his answer. That depended. She didn't ask what it depended on, she had no desire to continue the conversation. Her lack of interest in it increased from second to second, but her partner in the conversation didn't sense that at all, he was ready for a nice little chat. Depending on what her intentions had been, she could be proud of the result or not. My intentions? she asked with her most innocent expression. Her visitor took care of that silly question with a brief motion of his hand. If she'd intended – just as an assumption – a fatal outcome, then the gents she'd sent off to achieve that result were just a little bit, a very little bit, too weak. If on the other hand she'd merely needed a convincing excuse to take a breather from the absurd life that we all lead, then the greatest respect was due! She'd played a very risky game, that was no sham battle she'd let herself in for, but in any case, she could be really proud of, well, yes, of her victory.

But . . . she says, and her pathologist politely inclines his head in order to hear what she's going to reply. When she fails to complete the sentence, he does it for her: But there was no hidden intent there? She nods, not very convincingly, as she herself is aware.

My dear lady, her well-mannered guest then says, we don't even want to get onto that level of negotiation. Neither of us needs that. If there's anything that doesn't have the least influence on what we do or don't do or what happens to us, it's doubtless our intentions, don't you agree?

So he knows about the powers that do have an influence?

One could say that. Based on the outcome, if he were permitted to bring that in. At the beginning of his career, he himself had to wonder, sometimes, at all the things we humans resort to, just to achieve that outcome. You wouldn't believe it.

You mean . . .

I mean what we've been chatting about the whole time,

death. Doesn't it amuse you as well that it's so difficult for people to say that plain word in this, of all places?

It occurred to me.

Well, there you are.

But since you can't avoid it – why should you make a special effort to bring it about?

That question seems somewhat strange coming from your mouth, if I may say so, answers her pale visitor, who, it only now occurs to her, hasn't given her his name, a curious omission considering his otherwise overly correct behavior. But I forgot. You haven't yet fully regained your faculties. But here's one thing you can't argue with: since times long past, literature has been full of tedious descriptions of those efforts made by people lusting for death.

She can't argue with that.

And therefore the place where all those tremulous attempts by those poor souls end up is the very place where one is closest to reality. And – can't she imagine – that someone who would want to be very close to reality would find his workplace precisely there?

Yes, yes, of course. She can imagine that. Totally.

A workplace that did not permit the least self-deception?

That as well, certainly. Although ...

Although self-deception is one of the mechanisms of life? Of survival?

Well, yes, if he wanted to put it that way.

He? Want to? Oh, no. He doesn't want to put it that way, but all those who are still living do want it that way, are forced to. Well, then – as God ordains. *Chacun à son goût*, as we French say. Sooner or later everyone learns the truth, every single one of those poor deceivers and self-deceivers. We can depend on it.

She resists the temptation to find out which form of the

plural her guest has just used. Does he mean the truth that every human being must die?

That too. But first and foremost, honored lady, the truth about whether there's anything among the so-called mortal remains, anything that those destined for death have made of themselves during their lifetimes, that deserves to be saved. Saved by death, you understand. At that point, some of them experience – should the word be applicable here – a nasty surprise. Well. He's chatted long enough, has to leave, work can't be put off.

She doesn't stop him. Barely manages to avoid having her hand kissed. "Are you cold?" "A little." "I'll put the blanket over your feet, would that help?" "Very attentive of you, thank you very much."

The Professor, who enters, has met her guest in the corridor. "You've just had an important visitor. He's a very respected specialist, our colleague."

"Of what, Professor?"

"What do you think? For his investigations into bacteria and their growth requirements. If anyone's going to identify them, he's the one. You have no idea how many patients he's saved already. All that's left for us to do is to inject the drug that will kill the germs in question. He goes after them like someone who's obsessed with the hunt. He's developed an almost personal hatred toward them. And it's a real blow to him if it turns out he's taken too long."

"And the fatal outcome couldn't be avoided. That's a blow to him?"

"He can actually go into a rage."

"In other words he loves life?"

"That is, if you'll excuse my saying so, a somewhat curious formulation to apply to my friend. Perhaps I'd put it this way: He fights with death."

"May I ask you something, Herr Professor? Do you love life?"

"Yes."

But anyway, the reason he's come is to inform the patient of several changes that are going to be made. Starting tomorrow they're going to discontinue the intravenous feedings. A bland statement, after which he pauses to give her an opportunity to object. When she remains silent, he assumes her role: Yes, of course, it's clear that she'll have to get used to eating normally again, but in general that goes surprisingly quickly. After a few days she won't be able to imagine that she'd been getting along without food.

For the moment, however, she can't imagine how she's going to be able to eat the whole slice of bread that Sister Evelyn has placed on her bedside table with a flourish. "White bread," she said secretively at the same time. Before that she'd pulled the needle out of her arm where it had been taped in place for weeks and draped it and the I.V. tubing over the bottle. So, she's gradually turning into a real human being again. No more of the elixir of life flows into her veins. She has to let herself be propped up a little in order to spoon out her own soup. It turns out that her mouth doesn't know what to make of the soup, mainly because there's no longer an organ for taking in nourishment at the place where the doctors presume her stomach to be – it wasn't able to keep itself in working order, since it wasn't called on for such a long time. A highly informative discovery. The bread scratches her throat more than she can stand, after three bites she puts it back and firmly declares she has no appetite. That'll come eventually, she's told, but meanwhile she has to eat. Especially things that have iron, her iron stores are depleted, no wonder after the blood loss.

You bring blackcurrant juice, homemade vegetable soup,

and tender, stewed chicken legs. That eating's a torture is something you can't believe, of course, eventually I'm going to get on the nerves of even the most good-natured person, but who am I supposed to tell how stressful it is, getting back to health? Everyone seems to consider it obvious that she'd want to walk again, and she would indeed want to, if she hadn't totally forgotten how to, and if Janine, the brown-skinned physiotherapist, whose African father was separated from his German wife years ago thanks to complicated political circumstances, just wouldn't ask her to do so much. She doesn't merely demand that she sit on the edge of the bed, but that she get up as well, stand beside the bed, and then, on her arm of course, even take a step, then another one, which means that she'll have to take those two steps in the opposite direction before she can finally let herself fall into bed again, exhausted and bathed in sweat. Janine promises that she'll come twice a day from now on.

The nursing unit has no clean patient gowns, the senior surgeon prolongs his visit and positions himself at the foot of her bed in order to clarify a few things for her.

The hospital, she learns, is a mirror image of society, and this one happens to be an impoverished society, even though nobody would admit that. "To put it in plain words," says the senior surgeon, "we don't have the money to buy even the most basic necessities, and that accounts for the fact that we're short of bed linens, towels, and, of course, gowns as well. And that's not even mentioning certain injectable drugs or home-grown gloves." I'd witnessed my share of the funny business with them. "We're forced to save," says the senior surgeon. "A production-sector firm has to fulfill its production plan, we have to fulfill our do-without plan. Luckily, our Chief is well thought of higher up, and when things get too bad, he goes over and bangs on the table."

A little sneaky, but just to investigate certain rumors, she asks him whether her apparently very expensive medicine is kept on hand.

The senior surgeon snorts. "You really shouldn't hear this," he tells her, "but I'm sick and tired of all this secrecy stuff anyway. Of course we had to get the drug from the West. And because we needed it in a big hurry, the Ministry of Health sent their courier, who has a permanent visa, over to West Berlin on the S-bahn, where he bought the drug, caught the next train back, we received a call, our messenger was waiting at the station with an ambulance and brought the medicine back to us with siren blaring. And none of us could guarantee that it was going to get here on time. I've never seen the Chief so jumpy."

"Aha," she says, "so that's the way it was. But one more question. Would anyone who needed it get that medicine?"

"Oh, yes," says the senior surgeon. He can vouch for that. If it really came down to needing it, the money would be made available from some special fund. "Then we'd have to economize somewhere else. And do you know what the result of that is? We all turn into the world's champion improvisers. Our colleagues who leave here cause a sensation over there with their ability to turn dross into gold."

"Like the poor miller's daughter in the fairy tale," she says. Then she asks him why he really didn't want to have a garden, too, like his Chief, who is almost as famous a rose breeder as he is a surgeon. The senior surgeon is still with the poor miller's daughter and doesn't understand the question. He can hardly believe that before the very first operation, a long time ago, she'd heard him say he absolutely did not want a garden. Of course he doesn't remember, before operations they talked about trivial things as a diversion, while their nervous systems were being switched over to strict concentration. But that's right, a garden would be the last thing he'd want. If for no other reason, because the Chief gets on their nerves with his different types of roses. His hobby? Now she's going to laugh. He collects coins. And along the way, you become a historian.

"And what does the historian have to say about the present?"

He searches vainly for a comparison.

"That unpleasant?"

"Even more so. But we humans are blind and that's our good fortune."

"And you make the blind walk," she says, and he: "Quite right, Madame. Nothing more useful has occurred to me. You, however, it appears to me, want to make the blind see. No wonder that sometimes you get the pins knocked out from under you."

"Does that diagnosis belong to your specialty?"

"To the specialty of common knowledge of people, I should think."

"Now you're laughing up your sleeve at this incorrigibly naïve person."

"You misunderstand me. Why shouldn't the likes of us long for the time when wishes still helped and your miller's daughter spun straw into gold?"

"Not all fairy tales end happily for those involved. But to your relief, I've been cured."

"Indeed. That's something we'll let you know at the proper time. Keep in mind that some illnesses are very recalcitrant. But I'm tiring you. I wish you a restful night."

As the darkness comes on, slowly and late, because we're approaching the summer solstice, she imagines the senior surgeon sitting in front of his coin collection, examining individual pieces with his loupe, and a terrible desolation floods over her. Everything has its price, she thinks, and all-consuming boredom is the price for the inner calm of the uninvolved. But maybe she was the last person who should pass judgment on that.

Then, in the segment of the sky she can see, after all those rainy weeks, there's a sunset. Her color-deprived eyes can scarcely comprehend the drama. And all of that's supposed to be pure extravagance, not meant for anyone special, not put on by anyone for anyone. That's something Sister Thea doesn't believe for a minute, anyone who could believe that must be very dim-witted. At any rate, she's happy that she knows whom she can thank for such a sunset and for a lot more besides.

Sister Thea has orders to remove the drains as well, "Finally this bit of housekeeping's over, the dear God has known for a long time how many holes a person needs, right? The other ones we'll just tape shut. I'll throw the tubes away and with pleasure. It won't be much longer now until you can turn on your side whenever you like."

"And even sleep on my side?" "Why not?" "Unbelievable, Sister Thea. There are some things you just forget how to do here. Oh, by the way, do you know what I just heard on my little radio? Scientists are working on genetic manipulations that will make cows produce human milk."

"I'll drink to that," says Sister Thea, who's not without a sense of humor. Would she call it a sin? Yes, she says with complete conviction. Yes, and yes again.

She'd put the word "sin" on the list of lost words that need to be found again, she tells Kora Bachmann, who thinks about it briefly, then makes her doubts known. "Sin" is, for her, one of those words that enslave people. She's learned a little about Greek mythology in the meantime. Hades interested her. She's already wondered where the patient's consciousness disappears to when she's put her to sleep.

Hopefully not to Hades, Kora.

Because then they'd be dead. But there are still those souls that hover along the borderline, no longer alive but not quite dead. And who listen to the singer Orpheus as he tries to sing his wife Eurydice free from the dead. That power of song, you know what I mean. Everything wild stops when he sings. Sisyphus sits down on his rock. The hound of hell, Cerberus, stops barking. The judges of the dead break into tears. Art as the means of taming the wild impulses of mankind, it's something to think about.

But Eurydice has to go back to the realm of the dead.

Because Orpheus can't control himself and looks back at her. Don't you think it's a wise thing that the living should not look into the eyes of the dead?

And why shouldn't they do that?

Because that gaze could make them incapable of living.

You mean that the realm of the dead might appear tempting?

Or the realm of the living might repel them. I've observed you, I've listened to you, too, sometimes when you're sleeping. You were off wandering in peculiar places.

With you, Kora. But you don't have to know that. You've undertaken to bring me back?

In case you haven't yet really arrived.

Have I arrived? she asks herself after Kora has left. Do I want to arrive? Not only take in the food of the living but find it appetizing as well? You watch critically and suspiciously as I tediously force down the nice, soft cream of wheat you've brought me. Spoonful by spoonful. Baby food. Just don't tell me again that nobody can make cream of wheat like your grandmother.

It would never have occurred to my grandmother that life could revolt her. Or that death would tempt her. She was too poor and had three children. Anyway, have you thought about Urban?

No, you say. You stopped thinking about Urban and the likes of him years ago and you'd recommend I do the same. It doesn't get you anywhere.

But maybe it does. For instance, what's the slender thread that ties me and Urban together? Did the thought ever occur to you that death can also be the best hiding place? That it might not be despair but cowardice that drives someone to it?

Who? Urban?

Urban, for instance. That he simply didn't have the courage to go on living. Would have been laborious, or don't you think so?

But his cynicism has always saved him.

For a long time, yes. Not always, as you see. The grain of hope that was still in him, that was his weak point, his fig leaf, if you get what I mean. That's where the spear could find an opening. He failed to kill off all hope in time. That's what did him in.

Indeed, he'd once strongly recommended that to her. Didn't take his own advice, apparently wasn't able to. Hope as a weak spot. Hadn't he expressed it just that way? And wasn't that the very last time she'd seen him? In the foyer in front of the conference room. At the break, during which a sumptuous buffet was supposed to put them in a good frame of mind for the second, decisive part of the meeting, whose course – that had become clear – Urban was directing, a sort of crucial test in which he had to prove himself. It was after the wild speech he'd given. When even the corridor to the toilets was being watched by inconspicuous young men. She should have been outraged, but unfortunately she was saddened. Unexpectedly she found herself standing opposite Urban. She made a remark about the surveillance, but he could only shrug his shoulders: "Not my turf." "You people wanted to buy us off with smoked-salmon sandwiches," she'd said. The corners of his mouth turned down. "A few of you have a higher price." She'd asked whether he'd written his speech himself and he gave her a straightforward answer. "No. At any rate, not all the passages." She asked, "Does it have to be that way?" He said, "Yes, it does." She said, "You're resorting to intimidation." And he: "If it gets us ten fewer opposition votes, it's worth it." "You consider it proper to condemn and exclude colleagues who, as you well know, are only demanding their rights." "I didn't say that," replied Urban.

It turned out that he really didn't consider anything "proper," or did she think he was that stupid? But if the very apex of authority was at risk, you had to do everything to see that things came out the right way. At that point he let them write whatever they wanted to into his speeches.

"But I, for instance, would vote against it," she said. "And a few others as well." Urban, tight-lipped, said he knew that and regretted it. They probably considered themselves quite courageous, but in reality they simply weren't thinking things through well enough. If that meeting, despite all their fears, were to proceed in a disciplined way and according to guidelines, then they would have won a few points with the leadership, then they could risk another step forward in a different area. Unfortunately that couldn't be expected now, he was trying to save what still could be saved.

"And what is there to save?" she asked.

Urban said, "The façade. At least for the time being."

She said, "So that's the way things stand in your estimation?" and he answered yes. She: "What do you still need the façade for?" He said, "To cover an orderly retreat." Or, he asked, would she prefer a disorganized rout?

After a pause she said, "You know, of course, what it means when you can only choose between two bad alternatives."

He knew. He advised her to give up hopes that could never be fulfilled, and, as well, that unproductive resistance of hers which apparently resulted from her thinking she could still change things. That was childish.

"The new Mephisto," she said. "Seduction not with immortality but with immobility. So you're giving everything up for lost?"

"Yes. At least for this epoch. It was unsuited to our experiment. We, too, were unsuited, we in particular." She didn't need to tell him it was a shame. A shame about the victims, whose number would go on increasing. Compared to that, the few people who were going to be shut out today didn't count at all. "They'll fall softly," he said, not without bitterness, "that I'll guarantee you. They'll even be thankful to us some day."

They went back into the meeting unreconciled.

Late that evening, she asks Kora Bachmann whether she knew that the pain one felt over a loss was the measure of the hope that one had had beforehand. Kora didn't know that. To abandon your defenses and follow the trail of pain, I tell her, would be worth the trouble. Would be worth living for.

Kora is entirely of the same opinion. We hold each other's hands again, the city glides by below us, but something is changed. Kora says, We dare not look back, either of us. I understand and finally I recognize her. She is the emissary who intercepts the souls not yet dead on the pathway to

Hades, snatches them away from the netherworld and brings them back to the realm of the living. You've managed to do it, Kora, I tell her, and she says, half jokingly, Yes, but it was a tough piece of work with you. I know that she must leave me now. She releases my hand and disappears.

I awaken feeling sad. It's a bright morning, Janine is standing beside my bed and announces that today we're going to walk over to the window. "Eight steps," she says, "we can manage that now." She doesn't tolerate any contradiction. While we're standing at the window, you come in with the Professor. Still having those private conferences? No. They just happened to meet in front of my door.

"Now have a look at the view so that you finally know where you've been the whole time."

The panorama is made up of city and gardens and the lake, which stretches off toward the horizon, sparkling in the sun. The way a lake sparkles in the sun, there are whole poems about that. "It's beautiful in nature, too," you say. I say, "Yes, it's beautiful."

"But you mustn't cry," you say.

"That," I say, "is in a poem, too."

TRANSLATOR'S NOTES

I am indebted to the following for their invaluable help in identifying the songs and literary allusions mentioned below, as well as for details of Berlin's topography: Christopher Carduff, Boston; Ian Heffs, London, and his Web site *www.geocities.com/northernrenaissance* (songs); Rolf Henssge, Dresden; Melinda O'Neal, Hanover, New Hampshire; Ingrid Rathgeber, Kassel; Eike Rathgeber, Arnold Schönberg Institute, Vienna; and John Urang, Chicago.

With the exception of *Symbolum*, the poems by Goethe cited below, like his drama *Faust*, are available in several English translations.

page 3   "... the spirit above the waters" ("*... der Geist über den Wassern*"): Alludes to the title of Goethe's poem "*Gesang der Geister über den Wassern*" ("Song of the Spirits Over the Waters").

page 4   "Man's life resembles the waters" ("*Des Menschen Leben gleicht dem Wasser*"): This line from "Song of the Spirits Over the Waters" actually reads "Man's soul resembles the waters" ("*Des Menschen Seele gleicht dem Wasser*"). The reader must speculate about the difference in wording.

page 10   "All that's transitory is just a metaphor" ("*Alles Vergängliche ist nur ein Gleichnis*"): From the last lines of Goethe's *Faust* (Part 2, Scene v).

page 16   "mussulmen": A word the Nazis used to refer to those concentration-camp prisoners whose will had been completely broken and who were no longer able to care for themselves.

page 22   "The future veils / happiness and pain / ... we make our way forward..." ("*Die Zukunft decket / Schmerzen und Glücke / Schrittweis dem Blicke / Doch ungeschrecket / Dringen wir vorwärts...*"): From Goethe's poem *Symbolum*, one of the "Masonic Songs."

page 33   The question in which the word "total" was "used up" was posed by Joseph Goebbels in a speech made February 18, 1943, at the Berlin Sportpalast, during which he screamed at his audience, "*Wollt Ihr den totalen Krieg?*" – "Do you want total war?"

page 34   "Comes the dawn, should God wish, you'll awaken again" ("*Morgen früh, wenn Gott will, wirst du wieder geweckt*"): From Brahms's *Wiegenlied* ("Lullaby").

page 34   "Why do you weep, lovely flower girl?" ("*Warum weinst du, holde Gärtnersfrau?*"): From the third verse of the traditional song "*Müde kehrt ein Wandersmann zurück*" ("Weary, the Wanderer Returns").

page 35   "Here crowns wend their way ... with abundance" ("*Hier winden sich Kronen in ewiger Stille / Die sollen mit Fülle / Die Tätigen lohnen"*): From *Symbolum.*

page 37   "A name with many associations": The myth of Kore (Greek for "maiden"), the young grain-goddess and daughter of Demeter, was gradually blended with that of Persephone, who was carried off to the underworld and permitted to return to the world only during the summer. The name Bachmann may be a reminder of the Austrian poet Ingeborg Bachmann (1926–1973), who was one of the more famous German-language poets in the decades after the Second World War.

page 43   "Let man be noble, helpful, and good" (*"Edel sei der Mensch, hilfreich und gut"*): The first line of Goethe's poem *"Das Göttliche"* ("The Divine").

page 62   "Build up, build up" (*"baut auf, baut auf"*): From the *Aufbaulied,* the "Building Song," composed during the East German Communist era by Paul Dessau. Bertolt Brecht's words have to do with kicking out the residual vermin of capitalism. The words *"bau auf"* occur also in a song of the FDJ, the East German Youth movement, and in one verse are repeated four times in a row, giving a two-syllable repetitive chant reminiscent of *"Sieg Heil!"*

page 63   "Named, tamed" (*"Bennant, gebannt"*): A play on the German saying *"Gefahr erkannt, Gefahr gebannt,"* meaning "a danger recognized is a danger prevented."

page 65 "You again fill forest and valley" (*"Füllest wieder Busch und Tal"*): From Goethe's poem *"An den Mond"* ("To the Moon").

page 62 "Now finally giveth / my soul release" (*"Lösest endlich auch einmal / Meine Seele ganz"*): From "To the Moon."

page 66 "And so he journeys with his light by night / down into the mine" (*"Und so fährt er mit dem Licht bei der Nacht / ins Bergwerk ein"*): From the *Bergmannslied,* a traditional German miners' song widely published by the mid 1700s.

page 67 "I once possessed / that which is so precious" (*"Ich besaß es doch einmal / Was so köstlich ist"*) and "now, to my torment / never can forget" (*"Daß man doch zu seiner Qual / Nimmer es vergißt"*): From "To the Moon."

page 73 "homunculus": In *Faust* (Part 2, Scene 11), the tiny humanoid created in the laboratory by Faust's assistant, Wagner. The growing homunculus accuses Mephistopheles of being a creature of the gloomy north and offers to light his way toward southern, classical lands.

page 77 The *Völkischer Beobachter* ("The Popular Observer") was a rabid, anti-Semitic newspaper founded in 1923 by the Nürnberg Gauleiter, Julius Streicher.

page 81 "Is there a devil that always wills good and always does evil?" (*"Es auch einen Teufel gibt, der stets das Gute will und stets das Böse schafft?"*): A play on Mephistopheles' line from *Faust* (Part 1, Scene 11): "I am the spirit who wills evil and does good."

page 81 "the Rajk trial": During the Stalinist purges in Hungary, László Rajk (1909–1949), Hungary's foreign minister and an outspoken critic of the country's Communist Party, was convicted as a Western spy and sentenced to death by hanging.

page 82 "Never fail to exercise the power of goodness" (*"Versäumt nicht zu üben / Die Kräfte des Guten"*); "Here crowns wend their way ... with abundance" (*see note to page 36*); "We bid you hope" (*"Wir heißen euch hoffen"*): All from Goethe's *Symbolum*.

page 82 "He who wants to live must fight. . . . And he who does not have the will to fight in this world of eternal conflict does not deserve to live": Compare *"Wer leben will, der kämpfe also, und wer nicht streitem will in dieser Welt des ewigen Ringens, verdient das Leben nicht,"* Adolf Hitler, *Mein Kampf.*

page 83 "By the Well Near the Gate": The poem *"Am Brunnen vor dem Tore,"* by Wilhelm Müller (1794–1827), was set to music by Franz Schubert as the fifth song in his *Winterriese* cycle. The song is also known as *"Der Lindenbaum"* ("The Linden Tree").

page 83 "Up, up, to the battle, to the battle / we're to the battle born" (*"Auf, auf, sum Kampf, zum Kampf / Zum Kampf sind wir geboren"*): From a Communist song of 1919, with words by Bertolt Brecht and music by Hanns Eisler, honoring the murdered Communist icons Karl Liebknecht and Rosa Luxemburg. There was also a Nazi version with words by Adolf Wagner. An SS songbook of 1930 attributes the melody to a nineteenth-century soldiers' song.

page 87   "THIS IS THE POINT OF NO RETURN": In English in Christa Wolf's original.

page 92   "I have surrendered myself ... my one and only fatherland" ("*Ich hab mich ergeben / Mit Herz und mit Hand / Dir Land voll Lieb und Leben / Mein einig Vaterland*"): Song written in 1819 by Hans Ferdinand Massmann (1797–1874) during Prussia's War of Liberation, and based on a Thuringian folksong.

page 92   "BIG BROTHER": In English in Christa Wolf's original.

page 93   "He who will not hear must feel" ("*Wer nicht hören will, muß fühlen*"): Old German saying.

page 101   "... that old horse that's carried me across Lake Constance": In Gustav Schwab's poem "*Der Reiter und der Bodensee*" (1826), the rider, on learning from villagers that he has unknowingly ridden his faithful horse across the thinly frozen Lake Constance, falls over dead of fright at mention of the watery dangers he has evaded.

page 109   "All that's transitory is just a metaphor": From Goethe's *Faust* (*see note to page 15*).

page 115   "*Chacun à son goût*": "Each to his own taste."

page 119   "the poor miller's daughter": A character in the Grimms' fairy tale "Rumpelstiltskin."

page 126   " 'That,' I say, 'is in a poem, too' ": The poem is
Ingeborg Bachmann's "*Enigma*" (1966–67), dedicated to the composer Hans Werner Henze, in
which the poet repeats the line "But you mustn't
cry" ("*Du sollst ja nicht weinen*"). The line was
also used by Gustav Mahler in the fifth movement
of his Third Symphony, a choral movement
whose text is based on an item in *Des Knaben
Wunderhorn* ("The Boy's Magic Horn," 1806–08),
an anthology of German folk poems collected by
Achim von Arnim and Clemens Brentano.

ABOUT THE AUTHOR

CHRISTA WOLF is the most celebrated writer to emerge from the former East Germany. She was born Christa Ihlenfeld in 1929, in Landsberg an der Warthe, now part of Poland. The story of her life to age seventeen – she grew up in a middle-class Nazi household – is told in her memoir *Patterns of Childhood*. She studied German literature at the University of Jena and the University of Leipzig, and in 1951 married the writer Gerhard Wolf. She was an active and enthusiastic participant in the political and literary life of the German Democratic Republic from its founding in 1949 until its dissolution in 1990. From 1953 to 1962, she worked as a book and magazine editor, mainly for the German Writers' Union in East Berlin. In 1963 she achieved an international audience with *Divided Heaven*, a story of East and West Germany during the building of the Berlin Wall. Her later books include the novels *The Quest for Christa T., No Place on Earth, Accident: A Day's News*, and the short-story collection *What Remains*, all of which have been translated into the major world languages. She lives in Berlin.

A NOTE ON THE TYPE

In the Flesh has been set in Minion, a type designed by Robert Slimbach in 1990. An offshoot of the designer's researches during the development of Adobe Garamond, Minion hybridized the characteristics of numerous Renaissance sources into a single calligraphic hand. Unlike many faces developed exclusively for digital typesetting, drawings for Minion were transferred to the computer early in the design phase, preserving much of the freshness of the original concept. Conceived with an eye toward overall harmony, its capitals, lower case, and numerals were carefully balanced to maintain a well-groomed "family" resemblance – both between roman and italic and across the full range of weights. A decidedly contemporary face, Minion makes free use of the qualities the designer found most appealing in the types of the fifteenth and sixteenth centuries. Crisp drawing and a narrow set width make Minion an economical and easy going book type, and even its name reinforces its adaptable, affable, and almost self-effacing nature, referring as it does to a small size of type, a faithful or favored servant, and a kind of peach.

Design and composition by Carl W. Scarbrough